BEAUTIFUL STORM

Unfailing Love BOOK FOUR

MANDI BLAKE

Beautiful Storm
Unfailing Love Book 4
By Mandi Blake

This book is a work of fiction. The names, characters, places, and incidents are products of the writer's imagination or have been used fictitiously and are not to be construed as real. Any resemblance to persons, living or dead, actual events, locale or organizations is entirely coincidental. The author does not have any control over and does not assume any responsibility for third-party websites or their content.

Published in the United States of America

Cover Designer: Amanda Walker PA & Design Services
Editing: Editing Done Write
Formatting: Editing Done Write

Paperback ISBN: 978-1-7337642-7-8

Acknowledgments

Writing this series has changed my life in a number of ways, but the people I've met and grown closer to have been a blessing I didn't expect. They say writing is lonely, but I've found it to be the opposite.

I feel like I owe my thanks to the same people with every book. Thank you to my family for allowing me the moments I need to write the books I love. My author friends, Jeanine Hawkins, K. Leah, Christina Butrum, and a whole host of others, have guided me through this journey day by day. Without them, I would be lost. I have the best friends, Angela Watson and Jenna Eleam, who support me every step of the way.

The first readers, Ginny Roberts, Tanya Smith, and Pam Humphrey make all of my books better with their ideas and advice. My aunt, Kim Barker, helped me understand a little about what it's like to be a nurse. I owe a huge thanks to Amanda Walker for the beautiful book cover design and Brandi Aquino for her editing and formatting skills.

Last, but not least, I want to thank anyone who has read my books. I've received an enormous amount of support for these books, and I'm humbled daily by your kind words. Thank you for taking a chance on my stories.

Note From the Author

I always enjoy writing stories, but this book took my love of writing to a new level. I couldn't wait to finish because it was aching to be written.

Marcus and Tori are a classic opposites attract story, but they're more than that. Tori is like me in so many ways. I struggle to be understood, fight with myself, and often wonder if I am *enough*. So, this story is about learning to accept yourself. No one is perfect, and we're unique for a reason. It's time to embrace the parts of ourselves that make each of us special while working to be better every day.

Marcus is my opposite, but I adore him. He's a hardworking man of God, and his ability to love in the face of so many obstacles is commendable. We're all looking for love, and I have to believe that we can always choose to be better than our circumstances.

I hope you enjoy the great love between Marcus and Tori. Their story is special to me, and I can't wait for the next journey in the Unfailing Love series.

ONTENTS:

*C*HAPTER *O*NE

Tori

Tori massaged the aching muscles in her neck with one hand and gave a half-hearted wave to the nurses at the nursing station with the other as she passed. Only one woman with a phone pressed to her ear acknowledged her farewell. The others were wrapped up in charts and orders.

The squeak of her sneakers on the tile floor as she made her way for the exit was monotonous enough to almost lull her into the well-deserved sleep she craved. It was the end of her third twelve-hour shift in as many days, and she always reached her physical limit around this time every week.

When Tori reached the parking deck and flopped into the driver's seat of her Mercedes, she cursed as she remembered she had forgotten her end of the week espresso shot—the one she relied on like a crutch to make it home on fumes.

Forget it. The blasting radio would have to do. She'd done this dangerous dance before, and her loft was only a mile away.

As she drove, flashes of street lights and store signs lit her way home through the dark Chicago night. She turned the volume on her stereo higher and tapped her fingers in a rapid dance against the steering wheel as she stopped at the last red traffic light before her loft.

The commute to work was generally a breeze. She and her husband, Scott, agreed that living close to the hospital was the most logical option when they began searching for a place to move into together. Scott was a cardiologist at Rush University Medical Center, and she was a nurse in the Labor and Delivery Unit.

After she graduated nursing school, Tori first met Doctor Scott Wright when she transferred to the cardiology department four years ago. After running into each other in the sterile halls and taking second glances with each encounter, they had started up a casual fling that lasted for months.

When their informal relationship didn't fizzle out on its own, they chalked up the phenomenon to natural staying power and decided to go for broke. Neither of them had much to offer a relationship, and they both understood the demands of the long work hours that come with being successful in the medical field. Scott proposed within six months, and they were married in two more.

Tori wouldn't have described it as a whirlwind romance simply because the romance part wasn't something either of them subscribed to. She and Scott were practical people, and romance wasn't practical.

She pulled into the parking garage, parked her Mercedes, and continued on autopilot until she was walking through her door without much recollection of how she had gotten to that point. No matter how tired she was, toeing off her work shoes at the door was automatic. Those things didn't come past the entry alcove. There weren't many things more disgusting than a hospital floor.

Tori had taken two steps into the living room before she remembered to grab her phone from her purse. Throwing her head back in exasperation, she turned and backtracked to retrieve the device.

She didn't get many calls, but working in the medical field was enough to understand that sometimes being able to communicate when needed could be the difference between life and death. As usual, only a text from Scott lit up her screen.

Text when you get home.

Tori fired off a simple response and moved toward the paradise that awaited her in the form of a warm shower. Scrubbing the grime and foreign bodily fluids from her skin was always her favorite part of the day. Other women relished taking off their bra at the end of the day, but her release was the well-earned cleansing.

She'd changed her shift to three twelves a few months ago in the hopes that she'd be able to see more of Scott. Most of the time, their work schedules didn't line up, and having four full days off every week sounded like a good way to catch more time with him. But once she saw that the open hours hadn't produced a different result, she took a clinic job during the week to fill the gap again.

Tori stayed tired, that bone tired that ached in the center of her spine and never let go, but at least she was fulfilled. Her work was certainly rewarding, and sometimes she rationalized that the success balanced out the lack of social or home life. The patients at the hospital needed her, and Scott could take care of himself.

The steaming water on her body was divine. Tori relished the burn and rolled her neck back and forth beneath the pounding current. After scrubbing her skin until it was smooth and a rosy shade of pink, she stepped from the shower and lazily dried off. She couldn't wait to fall into her memory foam mattress.

Wrapped in a terry cloth robe, Tori padded barefoot toward the kitchen for water, breathing deeply and smiling as she remembered that her down duvet was only a few moments from being wrapped in her arms.

Movement caught her eye as she passed through the living room and she let out a scream, clutching her robe at her chest as if she could prevent her heart from jumping out of its cavity.

"Are you trying to give me a heart attack?" She bent forward at the waist and breathed in deep lungfuls of air, trying to regain her resting heart rate.

Scott had been sitting on the couch with his elbows propped on his knees. "Sorry, I didn't mean to scare you."

"You didn't think I would freak out when I walked into the quiet living room to find someone sitting on the couch?"

The television was off, but that wasn't unusual. Neither of them had much time to keep up with a series or any regular shows.

"I was just waiting for you to finish your shower." Scott's clinical voice was kind as usual, but she heard an undertone of uncertainty. Why did he sound nervous?

She righted herself and realized he'd been sitting in a quiet common room waiting for her. Why hadn't he waited for her in the bedroom? He knew she usually passed out at the end of her last shift, and it wasn't unusual to find him in a deep sleep when she crawled into bed.

Instead of returning to normal after the unintentional scare, her heart rate continued to patter on with an added dose of adrenaline that gripped her chest.

"I feel like I haven't seen you in ages. How are things at work?" Maybe their normal small talk would ease her misgivings.

Scott stood to his full six feet and ran his hand through his graying chestnut hair.

Now, she knew he was anxious. Touching his hair was his nervous tic, and he hadn't made eye contact with her yet.

Scott was different in some way she couldn't put her finger on. He looked tired, but an unfamiliar glow lit his face. He seemed younger somehow. How long had it been since she'd really looked at him?

"I need to talk to you about some things. Maybe you should have a seat."

Her palms were starting to sweat now. Scott was thirty-four years old and had weathered medical school and many years in operating rooms with ease because of his notorious calm. Whatever had him on edge was something she shouldn't take lightly.

Tori stepped to the couch and slowly lowered herself into the plush seat. A sudden insecurity had her tugging at the hem of her short robe. She had no reason to feel over-exposed in her own home with her husband, right?

Infinite seconds had passed, and he still hadn't looked at her. Surely, the suspense would choke the life from her soon if he didn't say something.

"Scott, you're scaring me. What's wrong?" Her voice was a whisper she didn't recognize.

Tori had always been confident and assertive, two of the main reasons she had trouble making friends or connecting with anyone. Scott understood her, but that was probably because they were the same in that way.

She rubbed her palm hard against her bare knee. The pressure felt like proof of life, almost as if she needed to pinch herself to see if she was dreaming.

Finally, he looked at her, but his eyes darted away just as fast as they'd settled on her.

"There's someone else. I mean, I've been seeing someone. A woman."

Tori shook her head. She was confused and too tired to be jolted with adrenaline for a conversation like this.

Scott was having an affair.

Eventually, she was able to speak the question on her mind. "What?" The solitary word lacked finesse. She really was dipping into energy reserves. It was possible this was a weird dream she was having from her comfortable bed at this very moment.

But no. She could see Scott standing in front of her, pacing like a caged animal. "I'm sorry. I didn't mean for this to happen. I do care about you, and I respect you. I just…"

Her breath stopped with his unfinished explanation. This was really happening.

"Wh-what does this mean?" She was too tired to process what he was saying.

Shouldn't she want to know about the woman her husband preferred? Should she ask how long he'd been seeing someone behind her back? Who knew? Did their coworkers at the hospital know?

Tori couldn't voice the questions. She just sat waiting for… she didn't know what.

She felt the pang of betrayal, but the true hurt she should feel hadn't surfaced yet. Maybe she'd feel it tomorrow.

Scott pushed his fingers through his hair again and faced her. "I met with my attorney today. He has drawn up some parameters we both believe are fair—"

"What?" Was that the only thing she was capable of saying? At this point, she didn't even understand what she was asking with that single word.

"Since I'm the one who…" Scott had stopped pacing, and he propped one hand on his hip and the other cradled his lowered jaw as he contemplated a way to continue. "I know I messed up, so I told the attorney I'm willing to give you more than half of everything. I don't want this to cause a rift."

What in the world was he talking about? Did he really think she wouldn't be hurt by what he'd done?

"You cheated on me, but you don't want this to cause a rift between us?" There it was, that shock and understanding she'd been missing before. Her voice was high-pitched and shrill. "You've got to be kidding me!"

He held out his hands, palms facing her as if to say *easy, tiger*, but she would not be tamed. "Listen, Victoria—"

"No, you listen." Her finger pointed accusingly at him, she stood and raised her chin. "You're throwing away our marriage. You're the one who messed up here." She felt the skin between her brows crinkle.

Scott only met her fury with acceptance. "I know. I'm trying to tell you—"

"I can't believe this is happening." She turned and started her own pacing. In a split-second decision, she turned again and pointed toward the door. "Get out. I don't want to see you."

Scott looked at the floor and rubbed two fingers over his dark eyebrow. "We both know you can't afford to keep the loft." His voice was low, as if he hadn't wanted to say the words and hoped she hadn't heard him.

Tori's rage built higher. She made great money, and she'd always been financially responsible. But he was right. She couldn't keep it alone. The briny taste of iron hit her tongue, and she realized she'd bitten the inside of her cheek hard enough to draw blood.

"Really, Victoria. I'm trying to make this right. I'll get out of your way while you pack and find another place to stay. I've already moved a lot of my things out to give you space."

"Where are you staying?" She knew the answer, and she was a glutton for punishment.

Like the embarrassed little mouse he was, Scott didn't look at her as he whispered, "With someone else."

Her chest rose and fell with her heavy breaths. Scott had moved enough of his things out of their home to stay with *someone else* for an indefinite amount of time, and she hadn't even noticed. She pushed that thought from her mind to let the anger rule her.

She couldn't speak, couldn't stop staring at him like he was a stranger. In truth, she didn't know this man. She'd devoted as much of herself as she could to making him happy, and it hadn't been enough. Rejection stung in her throat.

Scott walked to the recliner and sat slowly but didn't relax. He continued to lean forward and examine her as she stared in fury. His calm was back, and she envied his unaffected position in this mess he'd created.

"I'm not going to leave you without enough to get by comfortably. I'm deeding the cabin to you. I've already told the attorney I'll move it to your name."

"Excuse me, but what cabin are you talking about? I'm not being exiled to the woods, Scott."

A headache was coming on strong between her eyes, but she didn't reach up to pinch the bridge of her nose like she wanted. She couldn't wait to hear his explanation for this one. A secret cabin? Really? How had she not known he owned a cabin?

"I had a cabin in Georgia before we married. I haven't been there in fifteen years, but I have someone check on things from time to time. It's a nice place."

No, their loft in Chicago was a nice place. She wasn't made for cabin life in the Deep South, no matter how *nice*.

"How gracious of you." Her voice dripped with sour honey. "You can expect my thank you card in the mail." She was being petty and immature now, but she didn't care. She was hurt in the worst possible way.

Rejection. The ache in her gut felt familiar.

"Don't be difficult about this, Victoria. I'm trying to do this right."

"Right. What would have been the correct way to dissolve our marriage?" Her sarcasm was meant to hit him like a knife. She'd never intentionally said hurtful things to Scott, but now she wished her words could hit him like a lightning strike.

"I'm sorry…"

"Staying faithful would have been a good start, or telling me how you were feeling before you cheated on me. If you needed more from me, you should have said something…"

"It just happened!" Scott's booming voice echoed through the room, and the silence that lingered after paralyzed her.

She'd never heard him raise his voice before. Her heart beat hard enough that she imagined she could hear its pulse in the eerie quietness.

When he spoke again, it was almost a whisper. "We met by accident. I wasn't looking to find someone like her, but it just happened. We had a connection from the start. A *real* connection."

Her cheeks burned at the truth of his missing words. The implication that she and Scott didn't have a real connection. Not like what he wanted now.

The injustice, the betrayal, and the death of her marriage all hit her at once. Everything had changed in ten minutes. How could this be happening? Their marriage had always been exactly what it was supposed to be—comfortable, convenient, and responsible. Love hadn't been a requirement before now. How dare he change the rules in the middle of the game!

Scott continued. "You know good and well that you and I don't have that."

There it was—the verbal slap to match her thoughts.

He rubbed the front of his shirt as if wiping off a speck of dust. "We're still individuals, and that's how we would always stay. I didn't know I wanted more until I met her."

Her. He couldn't even say the woman's name in front of Tori. Would it taint the blissful love that he and the unnamed woman shared? Or was he trying to spare her feelings with his vagueness?

Scott closed his hand into a fist and rapped a steady beat on the marble surface of the table beside him. "I woke up yesterday, and it hit me. I knew I had to tell you. I took the day off yesterday and today to get things straightened out with the attorney and move some things out."

He'd taken days off work. Doctor Scott Wright never took days off work. He hadn't even attempted to schedule time off for their honeymoon.

The magnitude of the situation hit her in the gut. Everything was painfully real, and her throat tightened up like a vise.

There was no way to change what was happening. She'd lost the fight before she even knew she was in it. She would have to accept it and move on. Tomorrow would be a killer.

Her fire had flared hot and burned out. Now only the sick feeling that came with extreme exhaustion lingered as she whispered, "I'll pack my things," and turned toward what had once been her bedroom.

CHAPTER TWO

Six Months Later
MARCUS

"Marcus, look at me." Mrs. Bradley's authoritative voice was the same as it had been twenty years ago when she'd been his elementary school teacher.

Not much else had changed. Marcus was still sitting in the principal's office because of a fight at school.

He huffed and looked up into Mrs. Bradley's aged face. The last twenty years hadn't been kind to her, or maybe it was the kids who weren't kind.

"Did you hear what I said? He punched another student in the face," she quipped.

"I heard you, Mrs. Bradley." The full implications of his little brother's school fight hadn't really hit home yet.

"You have to do something," Mrs. Bradley demanded, crossing her arms over her chest.

"Like what?" Marcus took the liberty of crossing his own arms and leaned back in his chair as Mrs. Bradley stood towering above him. He'd let her feel like the aggressor this once.

Marcus was just tired of being the parent. He was responsible for making sure his brothers and sister were fed, made it to school on time, and had a ride home, but he was also blamed if they did anything wrong.

Marcus hadn't signed up for the parent role. He'd never fathered a kid. But here he sat, in a parent conference with the principal because his little brother couldn't control his temper. This wasn't the first time Trey had mouthed off and ended up with bruises before it was over.

"You need to be there for him."

She did *not* just accuse him of being an absent parent… brother… whatever. His life revolved around those kids, and there wasn't any more of himself left to give them.

He leaned forward with a sneer. "What if I told you he gets it honest?" He'd spent many days in this principal's office himself for fights when he'd been in school.

She took the bait and threw it right back at him. "Would you believe that? You and I both know it doesn't matter who your parents are, Marcus. You never used it as an excuse for yourself, so don't do it for Trey."

Marcus' shoulders sank. He knew she was right. He'd never been a terribly unruly child or adult, but he'd caused his share of mischief. He'd be the first to admit that his bad-boy look hadn't done him any favors over the years. He couldn't keep up with the Joneses if he was king of the trailer park. Still, it could've been worse had he followed in his parents' footsteps… whatever his dad's may be.

"You're right. I'll take care of it."

Mrs. Bradley glared at him as she spat, "He's suspended for the rest of the day. I'll see you tomorrow, Mr. Channing." She turned away, dismissing him without a proper good-bye.

Great. What was he going to do with Trey for the rest of the day? Marcus had to get back to the shop. There was still half a day of work left.

"See you tomorrow." Marcus left the office and grabbed a wide-eyed Trey by the arm and stormed out of the building without a word.

In the privacy of the car, Marcus asked, "What exactly were you thinking?" He couldn't even look at Trey. His brother was only ten years old, and it killed Marcus to know Trey was growing up, turning into a rebellious handful, way too soon.

"Lee said Megan was hot, and he was gonna make out with her."

The outrage was a silent storm within him as Marcus calmly replied, "Well, we both know that's not gonna happen. Megan isn't ever kissing anyone." Marcus would make sure of it. He had enough trouble with his brothers. His sister, Megan, needed to remain the good one.

"That's what I told him, but he kept saying—" Trey let the sentence die, and Marcus knew the little pain in his neck had been defending their sister's honor when he punched that kid today.

Marcus rubbed his chin and sighed. "Listen, Trey, I get it. I really do. I wouldn't let someone say things like that about Megan either, but you can't get in fights. Mrs. Bradley only suspended you for one day because she knows I don't have a babysitter. Got it? It's bad for us if I can't go to work."

Trey crossed his scrawny arms and looked out the window. "I get it."

"I'll have to drop you off at Mom's." Marcus didn't add the condition that she'd have to be sober for that to even be a possibility, but Trey was old enough to know without being told, unfortunately.

"It'll only be for a few hours. Taylor and Megan are riding the bus home, and Brandon is getting a ride home after practice."

Trey just nodded.

Why did Marcus feel like he was constantly letting someone down?

He pulled his fire-engine red Mustang onto the gravel plot outside his mother's trailer and turned to Trey. "I promise. Only a few hours." Marcus ruffled the boy's hair and they both stepped out.

Marcus and his siblings lived in a small house a few miles down the road from their mother's dilapidated trailer, and they only visited occasionally to make sure she was still alive. Years ago, Marcus decided the kids couldn't live with her anymore. She was unreliable, neglectful, and toxic. What little Marcus could give them was better than this.

He pushed open the door to find his mom sitting on an old, brown couch in the living room watching CSI reruns. She was sober, he could tell, and he said a silent prayer that she could stay that way until Taylor and Megan could get here.

"Hey, can Trey stay here for a few hours until school gets out?"

Their mother pushed herself up on the couch but didn't stand. "Of course. Come here, Trey." She held out her arms as if her son would run into them.

The truth was, he knew Trey was afraid of her. They'd both seen too much of her destructive lifestyle to believe she was anything but harmful. When Trey looked up at Marcus with those pleading eyes, he almost turned and walked his younger brother back to the car.

If there was a sliver of hope that Trey wouldn't hurt himself at the repair shop, Marcus would be on his way to work with his brother in tow. But the auto repair shop offered far too many possibilities for serious injuries, and Trey wasn't one to stay confined to the office, no matter how tightly Marcus tried to chain him down.

"It's less than three hours, buddy. Just watch TV with her." Marcus patted his brother on the back and watched him move into the room to sit beside their mother—the stranger he'd never had the misfortune to know.

Marcus seethed as he drove back to the shop. He hated having to rely on their mom, even for a few hours. So much could go wrong in a short amount of time.

Would he ever get the hang of this parenting thing? The worry was the worst. Their safety sat on his shoulders, and he wouldn't be able to stand it if something happened to his siblings.

He prayed as he drove. It seemed as if all he did these days was pray. He needed constant guidance, and who better to ask than God.

Please let her stay sober, just for a few hours.

He hopped out of the car and sprinted into Brother's Automotive to find Cody hanging the top half of his body in the open hood of a Toyota Tacoma. "Nice of you to stop by, boss."

Cody Henderson was the last person Marcus wanted to spend the majority of his time with every day, but the guy knew enough about cars that Marcus couldn't afford to let him go.

He didn't waste time responding to Cody's taunts. Marcus had work to do. His office was dirty and smelled like grease and metal, but he didn't need a skyrise with a wall of windows to run a business.

Marcus hadn't gotten comfortable in his chair before the phone rang. He grabbed it and spat, "Brother's Automotive."

A woman with a proper Midwest accent responded. "Hi, my name is Victoria Sanders, and my car is—" Her deep breath caused a muffled sound to cloud the phone connection. "There's something wrong with my car. I'm stuck on the side of the road, and it won't do anything."

Marcus rubbed his brow. "Okay, where are you? I'll send a wrecker."

She didn't respond for a moment, and he wondered if they'd lost their connection. "Hello, Miss Sanders?"

"I'm here. I just… don't know where *here* is, exactly."

He almost laughed. She must be passing through. "Tell me what you see."

"Well, there's a shack across the road that says Salty's Peanuts, but I think it's closed."

Marcus jotted down the location on a Post-it note and said, "I know where you are. I'll send someone out there in about ten minutes."

"Thank you."

They disconnected the call, and he walked from his office into the main shop looking for Jeff. When Marcus didn't see the older man, he asked Cody, "Where's Jeff? I need him to pick up a car."

Cody stayed buried in the engine, working. "Had to leave. His wife had a tooth removed today, and he had to drive her home. He told you 'bout it, boss."

Marcus let his chin hit his chest. He'd forgotten they were super short-staffed today. "All right. I'll be back in a few."

He drove down Highway 18 wondering how he was going to move cars through the shop if he didn't have enough hands to work on them. The shop was just another responsibility that sat completely on his shoulders.

He spotted the silver Mercedes on the side of the road and pulled the wrecker in behind it. He might not need to tow it if he could fix it here.

Looking out the windshield, his eyes were drawn to a tall woman in pleated white pants, a matching, thin blouse that fluttered in the late-October breeze, and tall, skinny heeled shoes. Her straight, blonde hair sat neatly on her shoulders as if to accentuate her pristine persona.

This woman was definitely passing through. She was talking on her cell phone, gesturing wildly, and he resigned himself to take on the task that waited for him.

*C*HAPTER *T*HREE

Tori

"Just hang in there. This isn't necessarily an indication of how this trip will go."

Tori had spotty service out here in the middle of nowhere, but she was sure that's what her mother said. Her mom was always the optimist, and Tori appreciated the pep talk while she paced in front of her stalled car in the weeds that tickled her ankles.

"I know. I'm just ready to get this behind me." Among other things—like the betrayal she still felt after the divorce.

"This is just a snag in the road. Keep your chin up."

Tori followed her mother's orders and looked up to see a rusted wrecker slowing down on the road ahead.

"Mom, I have to go. The wrecker is here."

Tori rubbed her arm to fight off the growing chill. She'd expected cool weather in Georgia, but she hadn't been planning to sit on the side of the road for half an hour. She wasn't properly dressed for the occasion.

"Call me soon. Love you. Miss you."

"Love you. Miss you too."

Tori disconnected the call and still couldn't believe she was in the Deep South. She'd never been close to the area before—on purpose. She didn't understand the appeal. Where was the town?

Tori hadn't even heard of Carson, Georgia before her divorce, and now she knew why. She wasn't completely sure she hadn't missed it a few miles back. Her GPS wasn't certain either. She'd phoned the real estate agent she'd spoken with about possibly listing the cabin for sale to make sure she was still driving in the right direction.

She pocketed her phone just as a man in a faded uniform that may have once been a deep midnight-blue stepped from the truck. Safety-green reflector strips wound around his legs, arms, and chest.

Tori didn't move as he approached her. The man looked rough and scary, and she wasn't sure if he was there to help her or if she should be reaching for her pepper spray. His hair was cut short and his eyes were shadowed and dark.

His gaze traveled over every inch of her car but never landed on her. For some strange reason, she still felt the pricking in the back of her neck as if she were being watched.

When he was about three feet from her, she took a step back instinctively as he said, "I'm Marcus, the mechanic you called. What seems to be the problem, Miss Sanders?"

The introduction was so quick, she almost missed it. She was still getting used to her new last name, or rather, her old last name. She hadn't been Victoria Sanders in years, and it felt like someone she used to know. "I have no idea what's wrong. Isn't it your job to tell me?"

He turned to look at her, and she almost regretted the sharp tone she'd used. This man was intimidating, but he was here to help her.

Without a word, he opened the driver's side door and pulled a device from his back pocket and started connecting it to something under the steering wheel.

"What are you doing?"

"Checking for a code."

More like speaking in code, Tori thought. She craned her neck to see what he was doing, but she didn't want to hang over him.

After a few minutes, he unfolded himself from his cramped position beneath the steering wheel and moved around her to lift the hood and study the engine inside.

Tori followed him but kept her distance as she asked, "I thought you said you'd only be ten minutes."

Marcus continued turning knobs and reaching for wires as he said, "You're not the only damsel in distress 'round here."

She shifted her weight to the other foot to relieve the pressure the heels were putting on her arches. "You could've at least called."

"I was five minutes late. Are we seriously doing this dance?"

This meeting was starting off swell. "Didn't anyone ever tell you it's rude to keep customers waiting?"

"Didn't anyone ever tell you patience is a virtue?"

Tori propped her fists on her hips. "Is that any way to—"

Marcus stood and interrupted her, shutting the hood with a bang. "Car needs to be towed to the shop."

"Wh—what does that mean?"

He wiped his hands on a filthy rag he pulled from his back pocket. "It means you've got low fuel pressure." He stepped up to her, towering a few inches above her even in her heels. "And you get to finish off your road trip with me." His taunting grin begged her to object. "Get in."

He walked around her and sat in the driver's seat of the wrecker before she even moved. She took a deep breath and made her way to the truck, reminding herself she was tired and probably cranky because of it, but that was no excuse for his misbehavior.

Tori hadn't ever taken a ride with a stranger before, and she wouldn't be inclined to start now if she had any other choice. Sure, he was helping her, but she didn't have to like it. She was the stranger in town, and unfortunately, she knew this rude man better than anyone else in the surrounding five hundred miles.

Tori stepped up to the passenger door and pulled. It was heavy and creaked as it opened. The truck sat up high enough that she needed to climb into the cab, and she made sure to watch her footing in her new Jimmy Choos.

She tucked her body in as close as possible to avoid ruining her outfit as she sat. White was the worst possible color to be wearing in a greasy tow truck.

Marcus maneuvered the wrecker to hook up to her car while she sat alone. The bright side of this fiasco was that she hadn't thought about her divorce in almost an hour. The lonely drive from Chicago had fostered some of the worst emotions as she'd fallen into a pit of woe is me about her current situation. She didn't want to be taking time off work to travel to Georgia and sell a cabin.

Her life had been so comfortable. Why did Scott have to mess it up? She was still technically living with her mom, since she hadn't found an apartment she was sure she could afford close to the hospital.

When Marcus hopped back in the truck, he shifted it into gear and merged back onto the empty country road without a word. After a brief bout of silence, her unease mounted. She'd never met a more unfriendly person in her life, and it frustrated her that he wasn't talking.

"So, how long will it take you to fix my car?"

Marcus didn't take his gaze off the road ahead. "A few days."

"I can't be without a car for days. I have things to do."

He chuckled. "There's only one rental company in town, and it's small, in case you couldn't guess."

She pulled her phone from her pocket. "Do you have their number?"

"I do, but they're closed for the day. You'll have to wait until tomorrow."

She let her hands fall into her lap. "What am I going to do until then?"

Marcus just shrugged.

How frustrating!

"Will you drop me off today?"

He didn't answer right away, and she thought he hadn't heard her question. "I can do that."

The rumbling of the truck as they drove settled in around them, but she couldn't just sit here with a stranger without speaking.

"Are you from around here?" Tori asked.

His mouth tugged up on one side in a grin. "Yeah." That cocky smile was growing more irritating by the second.

He didn't even ask her where she was from. "I'm from Chicago. I'm just here for a short time." *The shorter, the better.*

Marcus gave the slightest nod of acknowledgment, and she continued. "What's the best restaurant in town?"

He turned to her with one eyebrow raised. "What kind of restaurant?"

"Sushi?"

Marcus laughed, deep and bellowing. "Sorry, angel, we don't have sushi in Carson."

"Not at all? What about Thai?"

He gave another deep laugh and banged the heel of his hand on the steering wheel. He was getting a real kick out of her naivety.

"Think simple southern, and you've got dozens of choices. Other than that, you'll have to drive about an hour for raw fish and curry."

Tori sat up straighter, thankful she would only be in town until she could sell the cabin. "Could you run me by the grocery store?"

"I'm not your chauffeur."

"I'm aware. I'll pay you extra. I'm just coming into town, and the place I'm staying has been empty for years. I'll at least need some basics for tonight."

He rubbed his hand over his mouth and sighed. "Fine, but I need to drop off your car and the wrecker at the shop. It's almost closing time, so if you can just hang out in the waiting room for a little bit, I'll drive you around."

They pulled into an old shop with a bold sign on the front that said *Brother's Automotive*.

They both got out, and he showed her to the waiting area without a word.

The room was sparse and smelled like metal, but she used the time to call her mom and leave an update.

A quote was painted on the wall before her in untidy letters. *"Am I my brother's keeper?"* She wondered what it meant.

When Marcus walked into the waiting room half an hour later, she was stunned again by his sharp features. His shoulders were broad, and his uniform was covered in grease.

"You ready?" he asked in a husky voice.

She stood and pointed at the writing on the wall. "What does that mean?"

He looked at the wall then turned to her. "You ever read the Bible?"

She lifted one shoulder. "A little."

"You must not'a gotten too far." He pointed to the wall as he opened the door. "It's from Genesis, chapter four, the first few pages."

He was still mocking her, but she refused to let him know something she didn't. "And just what does it mean?"

Marcus stopped in the doorway and turned to her. His dark eyes were intimidating, but she was a glutton for punishment. "It means sometimes you gotta do things in life you don't wanna do."

She turned his words over in her mind and looked back to the wall. "I don't know how you get that meaning from those words."

"Read the whole story one day, and you might understand." He stepped from the room without looking back to see if she followed. "You need anything out'a your car?"

"Yes, my luggage." When she caught up to him in her impractical heels, she asked, "Is that why the place is called Brother's Automotive?"

"No." He pulled her suitcase from the car and carried the bulky bag beside him as if it weighed nothing.

He was really going to make her work for it. "Then why the name?"

"I had my reasons."

She paused to look around at the large shop as he kept walking. "Wait, you own this place?"

CHAPTER FOUR

Marcus

Marcus had thoroughly enjoyed dropping the bomb that he was the owner of Brother's Automotive on Miss Priss Victoria. It was the biggest and most successful auto repair shop in town, and he'd worked hard to make it that way.

She caught up with him at his Mustang in the parking lot and stopped again. "Is this your car?"

The vintage, candy-apple red Mustang came as a shock to most, as he'd intended. The car was his best work. He'd rebuilt it from the ground up.

"Yep. Hop in. We're going grocery shopping." He gave her a wink before stepping into the car and starting the engine. He'd never get tired of that purr.

He pulled up at the grocery store and opted to sit in the car while she shopped. He hadn't quite figured her out yet, but Victoria Sanders was a fun puzzle.

Marcus took the time to check in with Megan.

"Hey, how's Trey?"

Marcus could hear the clinking of kitchenware in the background. "He's okay. Much better than I would be after spending the afternoon with Loraine. He's at the table working on homework until I get dinner ready."

His sister held a motherly instinct far beyond her thirteen years. Once again, he hated she'd been forced to grow up too soon.

He looked out the window to watch the gray clouds rolling in. "Keep an eye on the weather. This storm isn't supposed to be anything to worry about, but you never know."

"I will."

"I should be home soon. I'll keep you posted. Love you, sis."

"Love you too."

Victoria returned a few minutes later, placing her bags in the back seat, and sat uncomfortably beside him. Something had the city girl more uptight than usual.

Not that he knew her usual state. He'd known her for a few hours, but he could guess she was bothered about something. He just needed to find out more.

"So, what are you doing in town?" he asked.

"I recently acquired real estate in the area." Tori tilted her head to study the clouds as he drove.

"You bought property in Carson? That doesn't sound like a wise business move."

She whipped her head around to look at him. It would seem he'd hit a nerve. "Are you insulting my intelligence now? Where is this Southern hospitality I've heard so much about?"

Marcus huffed. "You moving here for work or something?"

"Oh, I'm definitely not moving here." She shook her head. "I'm a nurse in Chicago. I just took an extended leave so I could deal with this real estate matter."

That was unexpected. He was rarely surprised by people. "You're a nurse?"

"Yes. Why is that so hard to believe?"

He shrugged. "I just took you for a woman who doesn't get her hands dirty. Maybe a housewife or someone who works in an office."

She pointed a finger at him. "Watch it, buddy. You might need someone to remove that bad attitude you've got one day, and you'll be wishing you'd been nicer to me."

He laughed again. Man, this woman was a riot. "You might be right." He liked it when she squared off with him.

They drove for another few minutes before she checked her phone and pointed at an upcoming turn. "I think it's that road."

"Where are we going?" The sky was growing darker, and he could hear thunder rolling in the distance. The air was crackling with the power shift of the changing seasons.

"It's a cabin off of Widow Lane. It looks like it's by a river." She examined her phone again, no doubt checking an online map.

He studied her carefully, now more interested than ever. "I know the place. Everyone knows that place. Are you talking about the Wright House?"

Victoria's eyes grew wide at the mention of the name, and she asked, "How do you know about it?"

"It's not really a cabin. It's huge. Anyone who's ever been on Wetumpka River knows the Wright House."

The rain began pouring in earnest as they turned onto the driveway, and she looked as if she'd seen a ghost. She hugged her arms around her chest as the house came into view. It was a two-level log monstrosity that dominated the beautiful river landscape. Weeping willows dotted the riverbank and swayed in the growing wind.

When he stopped the car just outside the steps leading up to the wraparound porch, he turned to see her face shrouded in something more than nervousness. It was almost fear. She wasn't just worried about getting her expensive shoes muddy.

"Just stay here a minute while I take your bags in and have a look around. You said it's been empty for a while, and there's no way to know if someone broke in. Give me your keys."

Tori didn't protest, just fumbled in her purse and handed him the key. She sure was trusting. Maybe her fear weighed more than any reservations she harbored about his character.

He took her groceries and suitcase from the back seat and carried them through the torrential rain to the porch just as lightning streaked across the sky. They were in for a tense few hours with this storm.

The house was musty and stale, but the windows and doors seemed to be secure. He checked the power and water and turned on the heat before walking back to the car to let Victoria know the coast was clear.

When she didn't make a move to get out, he opened the passenger door and she shrank back from him. Sure, he was soaked and dirty, but he wasn't Michael Myers. "It's all clear."

She looked around but remained seated.

What was she waiting for? He was getting soaked.

When thunder clapped behind him loud enough to shake the ground beneath his feet and a flash of light lit the sky, she jumped and clutched her arms around her middle.

So, brave Victoria Sanders was afraid of storms. Interesting. He was sure she'd never admit it.

He found himself reaching out his hand to her as he said, "Come on. I'll help you in. Wouldn't want you to sink in this mud with those flimsy shoes."

His uniform was made of a thick material, and it was soaked through now, weighing heavily on his cold limbs.

Marcus watched her moment of indecision before she reached for his hand. He pulled her up and she stood close enough that he could feel the warmth from her body in front of him. Her hand was on fire compared to the icy rain that drenched his clothes.

The rain pelted her face as she looked at him in the fading light with eyes that were a bright, hazy blue and stood out against her dark lashes.

Victoria pulled away, dragging him by the hand toward the house. It seemed he'd underestimated her fear of storms. She clearly intended to keep him close after pushing him away all day.

CHAPTER FIVE

Tori

Tori wasn't about to let go of his hand. Her only lifeline felt incredibly vital as she sprinted up the porch steps in her soaking heels. She could sense him behind her—powerful and strong, but not malicious. He was a stranger she was inviting into her temporary home, but she had a sense about him. He looked dark and dangerous, but he'd had plenty of chances to show her his true self today. Beneath the brooding exterior, he wasn't bad.

Unable to weather the storm alone, she wasn't ready for him to leave just yet. In Chicago, she'd worked long hours and hadn't even heard most of the storms from the inside of the enormous, stone hospital.

Out here, in the wilderness, she felt vulnerable and unnervingly close to the natural phenomenon that could swallow her whole.

Tori wasn't sure why she was afraid of storms. She nor her mother could remember a bad experience she'd had, and it was maddening not being able to pinpoint the reason for her irrational fear.

It was a glitch. Probably part of the same hang-up that kept her from getting close to anyone. She was broken, and that was that.

They reached the door, and she moved to open it. She felt the weight of his hand in hers and turned to him. He was everything she should be afraid of—all darkness and secrets—but her instincts weren't screaming for her to run. He'd wanted to check the house before she went in. He'd cared about her safety. That had to mean something.

Maybe her instincts were just another broken piece inside of her.

Tori turned back to the house and stepped inside. It was much bigger than she'd expected. She'd let her mind run wild with the idea of a cabin, and she hadn't even considered that "cabin" only described the log exterior. In fact, the place was elaborate and stunning.

She took a step inside and felt a tug on her hand. Marcus stood just outside the door, dripping wet. She wasn't quite as drenched, since she'd made a mad dash for the door, not wanting to spend any extra time in the storm.

"I'll be right back. Let me see if there are any towels."

She left him on the porch and wandered around the halls and through the rooms looking for a linen closet. She found one on the second floor that had two musty towels folded on a shelf, and she grabbed them.

When she stepped onto the porch, she found him sitting in the swing looking out at the raging storm. Her steps were timid as she made her way to him, practically hugging the wall of the house.

She handed him the towel, and his fingers brushed hers as he took it. Why did she feel a rush of excitement every time their hands touched? Maybe it was the electrical currents in the air.

"Can I make you a sandwich?"

It seemed they'd reached some unspoken bargain that he would stick around a little longer. He knew she was afraid of the storm, and he hadn't made her admit anything out loud, and she was grateful.

"Sure." He kept swinging, and she moved back to the safety of the house and made two turkey sandwiches with avocado on whole wheat bread.

When she'd finished making the sandwiches and putting away the remaining groceries, she changed into dry clothes—a V-neck, short-sleeve shirt and yoga pants—before stepping outside to say, "Food is ready."

She really hoped he didn't insist on eating outside. She'd had her fill of the storm, and she hoped it passed quickly.

Throwing the towel over his shoulder, he walked toward her with so much confidence that she felt an instinct to knock him down a few pegs.

What was happening to her? She'd never felt that way about Scott, but then again, Scott wasn't a bad boy with a swagger that drove her mad.

Tori was surprised when Marcus set his towel down in the chair before sitting. His clothes were still soaking wet.

"I'm sorry I don't have anything you can change into." Well, it would be weird if she did.

"No worries. I've gotta get going soon anyway."

"Right." She bowed her head to her food and let the matter die.

After a few bites, Marcus examined the sandwich. "What's on this?"

"Turkey, avocado, cheese, and a tomato chutney spread. Why? You don't like it?" Would he really kick a gift horse in the mouth?

"It's good. I've just never had a sandwich with avocado on it." He paused. "Actually, I'm not sure I've ever tried avocado. It's good."

"How have you never tried avocado?"

He shrugged. "It's not exactly a staple in southern cuisine."

She chuckled as he looked around the house.

"Hey, listen. I have a friend who can probably drive you around tomorrow to get some things you'll need for the house. She's an interior designer, so she'll know where you need to go for all that decoratin' stuff."

"That would be wonderful. Thank you."

He didn't respond to her pleasantry and finished off the last bite of his sandwich. The rain had diminished to merely a sprinkle outside, and she realized she'd made it through this storm without the panic and paralyzing fear she usually endured.

"Marcus, I'm sorry for the way I acted earlier. I've been stressed lately, and I took it out on you. It's just... hard coming into a new place."

His deep chuckle was surprising. "You won't be a stranger long. Everyone's gonna know who you are soon."

"What do you mean?"

"You bought the Wright House. Everyone and their mama is gonna be asking about you, and news travels fast in Carson."

Her eyes grew wide.

He continued. "I won't tell, but I guarantee you someone will catch wind of it, and you'll be the talk of the town for a while. Just let it blow over."

She nodded, and he said, "I'm sorry too."

She knew that was the extent of his apology, but it was enough. What she'd first perceived as rudeness now seemed like just an innate quietness.

"You can call me Tori." She offered an outstretched hand and a fresh start.

He grinned. "But Victoria suits you."

She smiled back. "So does Tori."

He stood but held her gaze as he grasped her hand and said, "We'll see about that."

She didn't say anything as he walked to the door. He stopped, turned back, and said, "I'll send Sissy to pick you up at eight in the morning."

When he was gone, she realized this was the first dinner she'd had with a man since her divorce. In fact, she hadn't had dinner with Scott long before their relationship ended. It had been *nice* and not forced. She'd always had trouble connecting with people, but maybe it had something to do with the mystery Marcus carried. He didn't speak, yet she wanted him to.

She still didn't know enough about him, but despite his lack of words, something inside her felt as if Marcus wasn't a stranger anymore.

CHAPTER Six

Tori

Sissy showed up at Tori's door the next morning with a smile on her face too bright for the early hour. "Rise and shine, cupcake. We're going shopping!"

The dark-haired beauty was the complete opposite of Marcus, and Tori couldn't help but ask, "Are you Marcus' sister?"

Sissy laughed. "No, everyone calls me Sissy. My real name is long forgotten."

"So, it's just Sissy then?"

"Yep."

"How do you know Marcus?" Tori asked as they made their way to Sissy's SUV.

Sissy waved her finger in the air between them. "Oh no, the question is, how do *you* know Marcus? I'm dying to hear this story."

"There's not much to tell. We met yesterday when my car broke down, and I called him to repair it. I guess he told you that's why I didn't have a car today."

"Ha! Marcus didn't tell me anything. He never does. It's incredibly frustrating."

"It is! He's hard to talk to."

"Bless your heart. If you've been spouting off your deepest, darkest secrets while he sits there like a knot on a log, you're in trouble."

"What do you mean?"

Sissy grinned. "Marcus is a master at reading people. He listens. That's why he's so quiet. He watches even when he's not looking at you. He still sees you, and he knows things about you. Things you don't want anyone to know. He's got some kind of gift."

Tori's chest grew tight at Sissy's revelation. "You're joking."

"I wish I was. I'm a talker, and Marcus had the upper hand from the start."

Sissy made it sound like she and Marcus were close. Tori's curiosity got the better of her as she asked, "Are you and Marcus… together?"

Sissy laughed loudly in the quiet car. "Goodness no! I'm married! We've just been friends since we were kids. He's better friends with my brother, but we've always been close." Sissy thought for a moment. "Marcus has some pretty good reasons to keep to himself, and none of us blame him for being incredibly selective about who he lets into his life."

That sounded a lot more cryptic than she was expecting. "What do you mean?"

"It's not my place to tell you about Marcus' life. How long are you in town? Are you planning to stay in the Wright House? I mean, are you moving here?"

"No, no. I'm just fixing up the house to sell it."

"How did you get your hands on that place anyway?"

Tori shifted in her seat. "I'd rather not say."

Sissy smiled. "Good girl. You're learning fast."

They pulled into a parking spot in front of a boutique furniture store on a bustling street in town and Sissy stopped the car. "Let's get that house fixed up so you can get home."

Five hours, one meal, and a few thousand dollars later, Sissy dropped Tori off at the cabin.

Tori wasn't sure if she'd ever be able to think of the place as anything other than *the cabin,* as she'd been calling it, so the name would stick.

The sun was glistening off the slow-flowing river like millions of diamonds drifting downstream. Sissy grabbed a few bags from the back seat to carry inside and sighed as she looked out at the river. "I can't believe you live here. This place is a decorator's dream."

"It's certainly been a shock. I didn't see the place until I arrived last night."

"Interesting." Sissy watched her with squinted eyes. "So you bought it sight unseen?"

"I didn't say I bought it."

"You inherited it?"

Tori shook her head and opened the door to let Sissy inside. "No."

Sissy breathed a low "hmm" as she made her way inside and began inspecting the place.

They spent the next few hours talking about possibilities and paint colors for the walls. There were a few repairs to be made, but Sissy claimed to know some people who could take care of them.

Sissy looked at her watch and sighed. "Well, chick, this has been fun, but I gotta relieve the babysitter now." Sissy hadn't mentioned her family all day. Instead, she'd spent quite a bit of time asking Tori pointed questions. It was much easier to resist telling Sissy things than it was to keep her mouth shut when Marcus was around, and Tori wondered why.

"Thanks for your help. Send me a bill."

Sissy just smiled at her. "We'll talk about that later. I'll be back to help you with this in a few days. Give me your number."

Tori jotted down her cell number and passed it to Sissy. On her way out the door, Sissy turned. "Hey, you have any plans for Friday night?"

Tori gestured to the unkempt room around them. "You're looking at my plans."

"You need to come out with us. We're celebrating my friends' engagement, and it'll be fun. You can meet some people."

Tori rubbed her arm and bit the inside of her lip before replying, "I don't know."

"Oh, come on. I'll call you and we can work out the details."

Sissy left with a wave and a smile, and Tori thought about the fun they'd had together shopping. Tori hadn't ever been a friendly person, and she didn't have a single girlfriend she could call on a whim and talk to. But something felt different about Sissy. Tori wanted to be her friend, and that was a scary thought. What would it take to be a real friend to someone?

When Friday rolled around, Marcus called her around lunchtime to let her know her car would be ready by the end of the day.

"Great. Can you come pick me up?" Tori asked.

"I'm really not your chauffeur," Marcus quipped.

"And I really don't have a ride. Stranger. Remember?"

He huffed and conceded, "Fine. I'll be there at 6:30."

Tori threw the words "Thank you" back at him with a bit too much sarcasm.

"Anybody ever tell you you catch more flies with honey?" he asked.

"Why are we still on the phone?"

Marcus laughed before disconnecting the call, and Tori couldn't help but smile.

CHAPTER SEVEN

Marcus

Marcus called Barbara again to make sure she could watch his brothers and sister tonight. Taylor and Megan were thirteen years old, but Taylor was still unpredictable enough that Marcus didn't feel comfortable leaving him home alone. Taylor was going to be the death of him, if Brandon didn't end him first.

Marcus had known Barbara since he was a kid. He'd been friends with her son, Dakota, for as long as he could remember, and her daughter, Sissy, had never been too far behind them. Barbara helped him out a lot when he couldn't leave the shop to pick up one of his siblings.

Normally, he would just take the kids with him, but they'd all gotten themselves grounded for one reason or another this week, and he wasn't about to let them come to Jake and Natalie's engagement party. That would be too much fun for his grounded siblings.

After he showered the dirt and grease of the day away as best he could, he'd drop the kids off at Barbara's, pick up Tori, drop her off at the shop, and be at Rusty's by 7:00 for the party. If he hurried, he might be able to make it on time.

He pulled up to the house and ran inside. Taylor and Trey were playing a video game, and Megan's bedroom door was closed and so was Brandon's. Marcus would leave Brandon at home tonight since he was eighteen and capable of staying home alone.

Marcus showered in record time and rounded up the kids. When everyone was in the car, he noticed the silence and looked at the boys in the back seat. They seemed fine. It was Megan, beside him in the front seat, who was uncharacteristically quiet.

"What's up, Meg? You have a bad day?"

She shook her head and looked to Taylor in the back seat who shook his head.

"What's going on?" Marcus asked impatiently.

Megan finally spoke up. "Dwight stopped by today."

"What? You didn't let him in, did you?" Dwight lived about a mile up the road, and he was always stealing or into some kind of drugs, just like their mother.

Megan shook her head. "No, but Brandon went outside and talked to him."

Marcus fisted his hand and counted to five before he'd reined in his temper enough to speak rationally. "I'll be right back."

Marcus ran back inside and didn't stop to knock on Brandon's bedroom door.

Brandon leaned up from where he'd been lying on his back on the bed texting and said, "Hey, man."

"What did Dwight want when he came by today?"

Brandon rolled his eyes. "Nothing. Just wantin' to know where Loraine was." Brandon, like his other siblings, never called their mother *Mom*. They didn't know her well enough.

"What did you tell him?"

"That I didn't know!" Brandon threw his arms out at his sides but didn't get up off the bed.

"Get up. You're going to Barbara's tonight too."

"No way. You said I didn't have to go."

"If Dwight is comin' around, it's not safe for you to stay here."

Marcus wasn't above admitting he was afraid of Dwight. Not the man himself, but the threat he posed to the life Marcus was trying to give his brothers and sister. Brandon was at an impressionable age, and Marcus couldn't let Dwight corrupt him like their mother.

Brandon slammed his fist down on the bed and dramatically threw his head back as he stood.

Once everyone was settled in the car, Megan now crammed in the back seat of the Mustang with her brothers, Marcus said, "Buckle up. We're making a stop on the way to Barbara's."

Marcus pulled up at Dwight's house a few moments later and ordered his siblings to stay in the car before storming up to the door. Marcus had to knock two times before it opened.

Dwight answered the door wearing ripped jeans and a shirt the color of muddy water. He smelled like sweat and stale bread. "Marcus, what can I do for ya?"

"I heard you made a stop by my house today. Do yourself a favor and don't do it again. I won't hesitate to get the police involved if I catch you comin' 'round my house again. Understood?"

Dwight put his hands up in surrender. "Hey, now. I didn't do nothin' wrong. I just knocked on the door."

Marcus stuck his finger in the man's haggard face. "You've been warned, Dwight. I don't give a second warning."

Marcus stormed back to the Mustang and prayed for a way to get his family away from the curse that followed them.

Marcus dropped off his siblings at Barbara's and pulled his Mustang to a stop in front of Tori's house at 6:40. He smiled as he prepared to face her wrath for being ten minutes late. He stepped from the car toward her door but didn't reach the porch before she was closing the door behind her.

She wore a navy blazer over a pale pink silky shirt, dark-blue tight jeans, and short boots the color of her shirt. Tori was different from the women in Carson, but her uniqueness was growing on him fast.

He wanted to offer her a compliment, but he was sure she'd find a way to throw it back at him.

Forget it. A part of him enjoyed dodging her daggers.

"You look nice. Hot date?" Marcus asked playfully.

Tori smiled. *That was unexpected.*

"Actually, it's you." She looked at her watch in a dramatic show of checking the time. "You might as well drop me off at my car after the party. You might not have a problem being late, but I don't like it."

Tori walked right past him as he stood dumbfounded on the bottom step of her porch.

"What?"

"Sissy invited me to Jake and Natalie's engagement party. She said they wouldn't mind, and since you're going too, it only makes sense for us to ride together."

Tori was tucked neatly inside the Mustang before he gathered his wits and stalked back to the car.

Sitting beside her, he was acutely aware of the use of the word "date," and a sweat broke out on his palms as he gripped the steering wheel.

"So, it sounds like Sissy was a lot of help." A lot of good she was doing him right now.

"She's amazing. We have lots of plans, but I need to get my car back so I can pick up more supplies."

"Mmhmm." His mind was still reeling over how he'd gotten sucked into taking Tori to this party tonight.

She turned to face him with her chin held high. "Why didn't *you* invite me to the party?"

"Well, we might be starting off the party at Rusty's, but we'll probably end up hangin' out around a fire at the barn." He turned to take in her clean, pressed clothes and smiled. "Rusty's is a come-as-you-are kinda restaurant, and the barn is in a field. You don't look like the kinda girl who wants to get her boots dirty on a Friday night, angel."

Tori turned back to face the road ahead and shrugged. "When in Rome."

Marcus finished, "Do as the Romans do."

He'd pegged her for a woman dead set in her ways and better than everyone around her, but her willingness to meet his friends and the set in her shoulders that said she was determined to have a good time threw his theory in the water. He was rarely wrong in his assessments, but for once, he was glad to have misinterpreted the unpredictable Miss Sanders.

CHAPTER EIGHT

Tori

Tori felt a rush of adrenaline riding in a sports car with Marcus along the country roads in the dark. He rounded curves like they were meant to follow him, not the other way around.

He shifted gears, and she marveled at the precision in his movements. She'd been scared out of her mind to take the chance she had tonight, but it seemed to be working out. She'd gained the upper hand on Marcus, even if it was for a moment.

Two days ago, she'd never have pictured herself here, on a self-imposed date with a bad-boy stranger that set her heart racing. Everything about the night was new and exciting, and she found herself laughing to the roar of the engine. The sound caught Marcus' attention, and his shadowed gaze on her was enough to make her thankful for the darkness surrounding them.

Tori hadn't known what to expect from Rusty's, but she soon found out it was a restaurant surrounded by a gravel parking lot that looked like it could have been pulled from the movie *Roadhouse*.

The place was teeming with people at 7:00 PM when they arrived. There was a short bar in the back with a disco ball above it and a slightly elevated stage on the other side with a microphone stand and stool atop it. Few people were actually sitting at tables eating a meal. They were gathered close, smiling and waving with friends. She'd never seen anything like it.

Tori had been standing in the doorway gawking when Marcus grabbed her hand and pulled her around the groups. A feeling passed between them that made her want to pull away and hold on tighter at the same time.

"Wouldn't want you to get lost in here, angel."

Tori let him guide her to a table that had been pushed off to the side where people were actually sitting together, and she spotted Sissy standing at the end of the table rocking from side to side as a toddler lay against her chest. "You made it! I told you it'd work."

Tori chuckled and glanced over to find Marcus shooting Sissy an exasperated look that lacked malice.

Marcus shook his head. "I should have known you were the instigator."

Sissy just smiled and continued rocking the baby in her arms, while Marcus pulled Tori to a set of chairs. The crowd was a mix of men and women, and they were all looking at her as if they'd seen a ghost.

One of the women, a brunette beauty, spoke up. "Uh, Marcus, aren't you gonna introduce us to your friend?"

Marcus' face wore a bewildered expression, and he fumbled his words. "This is Tori."

The other two women rolled their eyes as the brunette said, "Come on, Marcus. Spill it."

Tori took it upon herself to finish the pleasantries. "I'm Tori Sanders. I just got into town a few days ago. I'm fixing up a house to sell. Sissy invited me a few days ago when we went shopping together."

One woman with sandy blonde hair and shiny amber eyes said, "We're glad to have you. I'm Natalie, and this is Jake, my fiancé. We just got engaged today."

"Congratulations!"

Natalie and Jake both shook her hand as the others continued to gawk. Marcus dutifully ignored their pointed stares.

The brunette who'd spoken earlier introduced herself as Lindsey, Sissy's sister-in-law, and the other woman, who was a tall brunette, but with shorter hair, was Addie.

It was a good thing Tori had excellent name recall because she met a handful of others at the table before a waitress handed her a sticky, plastic menu without so much as a word.

Tori studied the selections and finally asked, "Do they offer anything that isn't fried?"

Lindsey laughed and said, "That's the best part. Try the fried chicken."

Marcus propped his forearms on the menu lying in front of him. "You might not want to start off with something you eat with your hands."

She was meant to eat chicken with her hands? As long as it was common practice here, she didn't see any harm in doing it other than it seemed unsanitary. "Chicken sounds good." Tori closed her menu and looked up to find Marcus giving her a puzzled stare. Perhaps she'd found the upper hand again. She enjoyed surprising him.

After placing their orders, the women moved around the table and practically pushed the men out of their seats to get to her.

"So, spill it," Lindsey said as a few of the men wandered off to study the jukebox.

"Spill what?" Tori asked.

Addie tilted her head and smiled. "You just showed up holding hands with Marcus Channing like it's no big deal."

Tori looked at each of the women, including Sissy, and asked, "Is it a big deal?"

She wondered what the issue could possibly be. Was it her outfit? She noticed the others were wearing T-shirts and casual jeans, and she suddenly felt overdressed.

Natalie playfully slapped Lindsey and Addie on the shoulders. "It's not a big deal. We just haven't ever seen Marcus with a woman before. He's usually with—" Natalie dropped the sentence and began again. "He's just a loner is all."

Tori searched the crowd for Marcus and found him propped beside the stage looking back at her. He did seem like a loner, but who had they meant he was usually with if not them?

Lindsey patted Tori's arm and added, "He's a good guy. He just doesn't always play well with others."

Tori had to laugh at that. "We're not together. He just gave me a ride tonight because my car is being fixed."

Lindsey smiled as she patted Tori's arm again before removing her hand. "Uh huh, whatever you say."

The women eventually let the matter go as they started talking about Addie's upcoming spring wedding. They sometimes asked Tori for her opinion, and she found that she didn't know what to say. She'd had her own bash of a wedding with Scott, but it seemed exorbitant as she thought of it now and decided not to mention it.

No one knew her here. She didn't have to be the former Mrs. Scott Wright. She could just be Tori, the woman who lived in a beautiful cabin with a river view in the backwoods of Georgia. Tori, the woman who had dinner with her friends at a shabby restaurant on the outskirts of town on Friday nights.

Then she remembered that these weren't her friends, and she was still a stranger. She'd probably remain a stranger, if she could get the house fixed up soon and get back to Chicago like she'd planned.

A handsome dark-haired man stepped into the circle of women and immediately turned his attention on her. "Well, hey. I don't believe we've met. I'm Brian." He extended his hand to her with a grin that would melt the knees of any woman between the ages of seventeen and fifty.

"Oh, no you don't. She's here with Marcus," Natalie chided.

"What?" Brian looked around for the culprit. "Are you sure?"

Before Tori could speak for herself, Jake stepped up behind Natalie and wrapped his arms around his fiancée. "We're goin' to the barn. Load up."

Tori looked around as everyone rose from their seats. "But I haven't paid for my meal."

Marcus stepped up behind her and said, "I took care of it. Let's go."

She'd intended to pay for her own meal, whether she'd labeled their evening out as a date or not. She was a successful woman, but for some reason she couldn't find the nerve to argue the point. He'd paid for her meal, and that was that. It was actually a nice gesture.

"Thank you, but you didn't have to."

Marcus didn't look at her as he placed a warm hand on the small of her back and led her through the restaurant. "I know."

CHAPTER NINE

Marcus

An hour later, Marcus stood in front of a fire at the barn trying to talk himself into leaving. Barbara's house was just over the hill, but he'd have to take Tori to the shop to get her car before he could pick up the kids. It would already be pushing 10:00 PM by the time he could get the kids home and in bed.

Tori sat huddled in a group with the other girls in the bed of a truck. He really didn't know what to do with her. Right now, she looked like she was in her natural element, laughing and chatting with his other friends, but only hours ago he would've sworn that she was a diehard city girl who didn't belong here.

"So, what's the scoop on Tori?" Dakota asked. They'd been best friends since they were kids, and Marcus had spent more time with Dakota and Sissy's family than his own. Their mom, Barbara, had been a mother figure to Marcus when his own mom would decide to get high for days on end. Now, she was kind enough to extend the same open arms to his brothers and sister when he needed help.

"There's not a scoop. She's just passin' through." In truth, he didn't want to talk about her because he didn't want the others noticing her. "And she's not my type," Marcus said, but he knew the words weren't true as soon as he said them.

She felt like his *exact* type. He got the feeling they were the same in some pretty important ways. They were both sharp and jaded, possibly cynical. She was good at putting on a sweet face, he'd give her that, but underneath that sweet smile was a wildcat, claws and all.

Ian, another one of Marcus' friends, turned from where he was fishing. "What? You mean mysterious, assertive, and broken isn't your type?"

Natalie was standing beside Ian, and she swatted his arm as her brows drew together. "She's not broken. Watch your mouth."

Marcus smiled as he realized Natalie hadn't denied the other two descriptions, but he liked that Tori was mysterious and assertive.

But those weren't the things he'd been thinking about when he looked at Tori. He'd been thinking about that fire he felt every time he touched her hand or she looked at him with that playful smile when she knew she'd gotten in a witty shot at him. The way she never took his difficult attitude sitting down. The way she spoke her mind and didn't hide or deceive. She was real in a way most people weren't. She was unexpected.

This was stupid. He couldn't even stand her half the time, but the other half he spent wishing he could be closer. Marcus looked over the fire toward Tori and said, "She's a bad idea."

Now he was talking about her as if he actually had a chance with her and her fancy high heels and tailored jackets.

She wasn't a bad idea—if she would have him. The tequila that started his mom's downward spiral was a bad idea. Tori looked like something bright and good in a world of gray.

Dakota gave Marcus' shoulder a shove. "Hey, man, bad ideas can turn into good things."

Marcus cracked his knuckles as he watched Tori. Maybe he could take a chance.

He'd just have to convince himself he could make a decision for himself.

In his messed-up reality, he couldn't make personal decisions. Not while the kids were still his responsibility.

Brian threw a rock that skipped three times across the surface of the pond. "She's out of his league. Stop encouraging him." At least someone had the nerve to say it.

Marcus nodded and turned back to Brian. "She's leaving. Going back to Chicago."

Brian shrugged. "So your relationship has an expiration date. You don't seem like the marrying type anyway. I mean, you've already got kids. Who needs a wife?"

Marcus had heard enough reasons why nothing could ever happen between Tori and himself, and his gut was twisting at the thought. Why did it feel like everything he wanted in life was being taken away at once? He'd been putting his wants last for years without complaining. Why did this seem like an injustice?

"You're right. I need to get home." He found Jake and Natalie and said a quick congratulations on their engagement before he made his way to the truck where Tori sat bundled up in a fleece blanket talking in hushed voices with Addie and Lindsey.

He banged his open hand against the side of the truck just hard enough to get Tori's attention. "We need to head out."

Tori looked to the girls and whispered good-byes before standing and walking to the tailgate of the truck. She stood on the edge of the bed looking down at him, and he knew she'd have a problem getting herself down in those crazy shoes.

Marcus reached his hands up to her as she leaned down to brace her hands on his shoulders. He lifted her down with ease and steadied her on the ground in front of him.

It felt nice to hold her this close, to have her in his arms, but he looked away from her as Brian's words rang in his head.

"Come on." He took the time to grab her hand and lead her to the Mustang and open the passenger door for her. He felt a ripping in his chest when he released her hand, but he didn't react, didn't say anything, as he got into the car and drove away.

CHAPTER TEN

Tori

Marcus was quiet on the ride to Brother's Automotive, but that wasn't unusual. For the first time, she felt like something wasn't being said between them, and it was dampening her high spirits from the fun night out.

"Thank you for letting me meet your friends. Jake and Natalie are so cute together, and Addie and Lindsey are fun. I can't remember the last time I just sat around with friends and talked."

She was doing it again—word vomiting while he took in everything she said to analyze and interpret—but she couldn't stop herself.

She tried again. "Brian seems funny."

Tori turned to see Marcus' jaw clench tight in the dim streetlights, but he didn't respond.

"What's wrong?"

"Nothing."

He was impossible. She'd seen him open up a little with his friends tonight, and now the two of them were back to square one. "Would you like to come by the cabin tomorrow? I have some work to do fixing it up, but I could make us lunch."

Marcus took a deep breath and released it slowly as he turned into the gravel lot beside Brother's Automotive. "I can't."

The words strummed a familiar chord in her chest that ached. "You can't or you won't?"

"Both."

"I get it," she spat.

"No, you don't." He shifted the car into park with too much force and turned to her. "You don't know. You're leaving, and I have to get home." His gaze shifted to the clock on the dash.

"You're married, aren't you?" Of all the terrible things to happen to her, she would be riding around town with a married man.

"Good grief, no. I'm not married, but I have a lot on my plate… all the time. I have a life…"

"Whatever. That's fine. Thank you for the ride." Tori wanted to hesitate. She didn't want to leave because this was good-bye for good. She probably wouldn't see him again. But another, furious part of her couldn't stop the terrible reaction to his hurtful words. If he thought she would disrupt his perfect life, she'd make herself scarce.

Tori stepped from the car as Marcus called her name, but she slammed the door and walked to her car. Her shoulders were square and her chin was high in the air just as her mother had told her, but she felt wounded inside. She was thankful he couldn't see her face as she got in her car, found the keys in the cup holder, and started the engine.

Her tires spun in the gravel as she ran from Marcus—that impossible man who'd made her think she could be someone different in this new town. She couldn't say he'd led her on, but it still felt as if he had in some way. He hadn't pushed her away like she expected, he hadn't been impersonal like everyone else, and he hadn't left her… until now.

Tori drove back to the cabin without looking back. The mechanical voice of the navigation system was the only distraction from her thoughts of Marcus.

Tori knew it would be hard after her divorce, but this was a hurt she hadn't expected. She knew now that she wasn't made for marriage and relationships, but something had felt different with Marcus. Now, the realization that she would spend her life alone was maddening.

She was a loner anyway. She'd never had real friends, and her mom was the only family she cared about now. Pets weren't even an option for her when she spent so much time working.

Her anger hadn't abated when she arrived at the cabin, and she went through the house slamming doors behind her for no reason other than to release her fury.

She finally changed out of her ridiculous clothes, washed her face, and threw herself into bed. The sheets and blankets still smelled musty, since she hadn't gotten around to washing them yet. She'd been exhausted since she arrived from working on other parts of the house.

Washing sheets was one more thing to add to her growing list of things to do before she could leave this cabin in the middle of nowhere.

That wasn't fair. She loved the house. It was a certain man in town that had her fired up. This was all his fault. Tori was convinced that if he wasn't married, he was hiding something else.

She thought about what he'd said in the car. He'd said he had to get home, so maybe it was a pet. *Surely not.* He'd said he had a *life*, as if she didn't!

Then she thought about his mysterious explanation about the quote on the wall at the shop. *Am I my brother's keeper?*

He said it was in the Bible, but she couldn't remember where. Not that she had a Bible. She hadn't been to church since her neighbor used to take her on Sunday mornings so her parents could fight without her hearing.

Tori grabbed her phone from the nightstand. There was an app for everything, right? He'd said it was in the first few pages, so she'd just start at the beginning.

Propped on her elbows, she read about the creation of the world, animals, and people, and felt the power in the words. Then Adam and Eve were given the Garden of Eden, and they shunned their gift after being tempted by a serpent with a forked tongue. They were cast out of the Garden by God, and their shame and guilt was passed down all the way to her as she lay in this bed. Their curse was undoubtedly still alive today.

By the time she reached chapter four of the first book, she was invested. When she read the telling of Cain and Abel, she stared at the words in fascination.

Am I my brother's keeper?

Cain was cursed and made to wander the earth after killing his brother, but what did that have to do with Marcus? He'd said she would understand if she read it, but she didn't.

The clock read 10:30 PM, but she decided to call her mom. It was only 9:30 PM in Chicago, and they often talked well into the night.

"Hey, sweetie."

"Hey, Mom."

"You sound down. What's on your mind? Are you having a hard time with the house repairs?"

Tori rubbed her finger over the hem of the sheet and sighed. "No, it's fine. It's something else I wanted to ask you." Her mom didn't prod as Tori thought about it.

"When did my fear of storms start? Did something happen?"

Her mom sighed. "I can't remember a time when you weren't afraid of them. I guess it started when you were a toddler, when you were old enough to know what was happening."

Tori's heart sank. The irrational fear that had shown its ugly head when she arrived here was ingrained in her. You can't teach an old dog new tricks, and you can't teach an old girl not to fear the thunder.

"Honey, it's okay to be afraid sometimes. Just don't let the fear rule you. Keep fighting until you know you're stronger than what you're fighting against."

Her mom was always so optimistic, but Tori had missed that personality trait when her parents' DNA was divvied up.

"Why haven't I ever been able to get close to someone? I mean, I love you so much, and we talk every day about everything, but why can't I have that with anyone else?"

Her mom's deep breath echoed through the phone. "Because you know you can trust me. After your dad left, you didn't trust anyone, and you still don't. I think it's been harder on you lately because of this mess with Scott."

"That's true."

"But you always trusted me, and I never gave you a reason to doubt me. When your dad left, you wanted stability in *every* part of your life. It was easier for you to overcome the sadness when your life was structured, and I did my best to give that to you. Now, I know I didn't do you any favors because the world and the people in it aren't always going to fit into a box. People are going to make mistakes, and when they do, you have a hard time forgiving them."

Her mom was right. She held grudges against everyone who wronged her, and now she was doing the same to Scott, even if he didn't care.

"Maybe it's time to start seeing people as human and flawed. You're not perfect, and you make mistakes too."

Tori thought about the passage she'd just read in the Bible about the beginning of sin and realized her mother was right. People had been sinning since the dawn of time, and she was no exception.

"I'm sorry I'm tough on people, Mom. It's not fair to expect everyone else to be perfect."

"Is this about someone in Georgia?" her mom asked.

"I don't know yet. I'll let you know if it is."

They said their good nights and the exhaustion of the day weighted heavy on her shoulders. She'd think about the rest of it tomorrow.

Chapter Eleven

Marcus

Marcus spent the next week wondering what he could have been doing had he taken Tori up on her offer to spend time at her place. He'd been a jerk, and he couldn't get it out of his mind as he watched from the rocking chair on the front porch as Taylor picked up sticks in the yard.

It hadn't helped matters that Tori had mentioned Brian that night Marcus had taken her to her car.

Of course, Brian was the popular one who women flocked to. He'd also never met a person who wasn't instantly his best friend. The guy had a magnetic personality, and Marcus was the opposite. If Tori was interested in Brian, Marcus had better just get out of the way now.

The problem was he didn't want to just step aside. He wanted Tori asking questions about *him*, not Brian.

Taylor made the last trip to the stick pile with his arms full, and Marcus signaled for him to call it a day. The benefits of having grounded wards were the extra chores to be done. Marcus was a master of thinking up all kinds of improvement tasks for his siblings when they were in trouble. They required more constant supervision while grounded, but he couldn't deny the things they accomplished.

The sun was almost set, and Taylor had gone inside to help Megan cook dinner, but Marcus didn't want to move from his comfortable spot on the porch. The thick November wind was uncharacteristically frigid this early in the year, but he huddled in his flannel and fleece jacket and weathered the cold. He'd done a lot of thinking about Tori in this chair, and he wanted to be left alone with his thoughts.

His cell buzzed in his pocket and he pulled it out to find it was Brian.

"Hey, man."

"Hey, what's up with your new lady friend?" Brian was anything but subtle.

"I don't know."

"Well, I do. Jenny, the waitress at Rusty's, just called me from her second job at The Crow's Nest. Your girl has been there since they opened the doors, and she's quite a handful now. I told Jenny I'd give you a call."

Marcus sat up straighter in his chair. "She's drunk?" Just like Tori to keep surprising him like this. Unfortunately for her, he didn't like these kinds of surprises.

"Yep. You better go get her."

Marcus disconnected the call and warned his siblings that if anyone moved a finger the wrong way, he would know it, and started toward downtown Carson.

The Crow's Nest was a shady dive bar in a bad part of town, and he dreaded having to walk in. His mom had spent many hours in that hole, and he remembered dragging her out more times than he could count. He refused to let Tori be a replay of his mother's mistakes.

Marcus didn't drink out of extreme caution against any kind of genetic predisposition to addiction. Plus, he always needed to be on his guard in case of an emergency with his siblings. They needed him more than he needed any substance. Not that he ever had extra money floating around for things like frivolous drinks.

The parking lot was packed when he arrived, and he checked the time to find it was only 8:00 PM. The night was just getting started for these folks. He parked beside the dumpster on the side of the building and made his way inside.

Marcus had his reasons for hating The Crow's Nest. If there was a place that haunted him and wouldn't let him have his peace, he was looking at it now.

Journey's "Don't Stop Believing" was blaring, and he searched for Tori through the haze. Once he spotted her at the bar, he kept his eyes on his target as he maneuvered around sweaty bodies and cigarette smoke toward her.

He couldn't help wondering how many of these people had someone at home waiting for them. How many of these people knew the real cost of a drink?

Marcus was tired of the highs and lows Tori caused him. How could she do something like this? Sure, he'd made her mad, but that wasn't a good reason to run off to a place like this by herself. He was furious. Livid that she would choose this place above all others to make him chase her.

Marcus was huffing in his anger, and the rancid smell of beer and sweat was enough to make him snarl.

Tori deserved better than this place, just like she was too good for him.

When he reached her, she was leaning over the bar, backside stuck up in the air, reaching for an empty glass on the bartender's side.

Jenny swatted her hand. "I told you to keep your nasty hands off my glasses."

He stood beside Tori seething for a few moments before she even noticed him. She looked different tonight in a T-shirt and jeans. Although, the jeans were probably a designer brand if he knew her at all. Her tailored coat hung out of place on the back of the dirty barstool. He liked the casual look on her. Even her blonde hair hung straight, instead of the subtle waves she favored.

"Oh, hey, you! What're you doing here?" Her Chicago accent came out in full force when she'd been drinking.

"I came for you."

Her eyes widened and she placed a hand over her heart. "For me? You shouldn't have. Although, you're real pretty to look at. I'm kind of glad you came." She tilted her head to one side until it almost sat on her shoulder. "Look at those muscles."

He caught her wrist when she reached to touch him, and his anger flared hotter. This wasn't her—not the Tori he knew and cared about. The one-woman show she was putting on was the main reason why he couldn't get close to her. She could do one thing, make one decision, and have him tied up in knots.

Marcus wasn't a fan of *anyone* having that kind of power over him.

He kept his hold on her wrist and leaned in to whisper in her ear. "You'd better stop talking, angel. You'll say more than you want me to know."

A gruff man in his forties stepped up beside Tori and put his hand around her waist. "Hey, pretty lady. Come dance with me."

Marcus was going to lose his mind before he got her out of this bar. The man was roughly the same size as Marcus, but all it took was a glare from Marcus before the man turned to the next woman and shouted the same demand.

"Are you taking me home?" Tori's brows were drawn together, and she looked pale. Of course, he would have to put her in his prized Mustang when she was bound to vomit.

"I guess I am. Remind me to have a heart-to-heart with you tomorrow about risky behavior."

"Aww, Mr. Chivalry. How kind of you." She even kept her sarcastic personality when she was drunk.

Good to know. He paid her tab and ushered her toward the door.

Marcus was tired of picking up after the people in his life who were slaves to their addictions. His friend, Dakota, wasted a year intoxicated after his girlfriend, Lindsey, left him. He only found his solid footing last year when Lindsey came back and they made amends.

Marcus sucked in a deep breath, shoving down the years of hurt. If only that were the case with his mother, who still caused him a headache on a regular basis.

"I read about your mysterious quote." She waved her hands in the air like an amateur magician getting ready for a trick. "You said I'd understand it, but I don't." She stumbled over her own foot, and he grabbed her arm to keep her steady.

"What quote?"

"Something about watching your brother." Tori waved a dismissive hand in the air.

Marcus' chest tightened. How did she know about his brother?

"I don't know how it means what you said it means. I can't remember what you said, but I know that's not what it means."

When he realized she was talking about the quote at his repair shop, he let out a relieved sigh. "Oh, really?"

"He killed his brother. Who does that? It was terrible." She stumbled against the Mustang, and he opened the passenger door to guide her inside.

She turned to him, finger pointed in his face. "I know why men take women home from bars, Marcus. They just think they're getting lucky. I haven't been out in years, but some things don't change. You're no saint."

He took a few deep breaths to calm his temper. "I never claimed to be a saint, but you're wrong, angel. I don't feel *lucky* tonight. Get in."

Tori's anger abated, and her eyes turned glassy with tears. "Men are pigs."

For once, he didn't know what to feel. The look in her eyes was crushing him, but she'd just insulted him. "I might not be from the same side of the tracks as you, but I'm not a pig. I'm actually just taking you home, where you should stay."

She sat down in the seat and looked up at him.

"Do you need to let it all out before we get on the road?" he asked.

Tori shook her head slowly and curled up in the seat. How could she be so frustrating and so cute at the same time?

She was quiet on the ride to her cabin, and he didn't wake her for fear she would get sick. When they arrived at her house, or what he thought of as her house—she intended to sell it he assumed—he got out and helped her stand.

She stopped before the first step of the porch and stared at the ground.

"What's wrong?" he asked.

Before the words were out of his mouth, she was vomiting in the shrubs. Marcus grabbed her hair and held her waist to steady her. This was eerily close to all those nights he'd looked after his mom before he'd moved out and taken his brothers and sister with him.

When they reached the door, she fumbled the keys and dropped them. She immediately leaned down to pick them up and fell into a heap on the porch. Marcus said a prayer for patience as he grabbed the keys and opened the door. When he picked her up off the floor and carried her into the house like a sleeping child, he wondered where it had all gone wrong.

Her skin was warm against his as the frigid November air whirled around them, and he shut the door behind them against the cold.

Marcus took a few steps toward the couch in the living room before she wiggled. "I can walk."

"You sure? 'Cause you looked like a baby deer stumbling around on the porch."

She wiggled harder and slapped at his shoulder. "Stop it. I'm a capable woman."

He was careful as he set her feet down on the floor and said, "I know what you're capable of, angel. You've been tearing me down since we met. Can't you give it a break for one night?"

Tori interrupted him. "Stop it, Marcus." Her tone was serious, but he wasn't backing down.

"What? You can dish it out, but you can't take it?"

"No, stop moving. I'm about to throw up."

"Don't just stand there. Where's the bathroom?" He looked around but didn't see anything at first glance.

She pointed down a hall, and he held her hand and waist as he guided her into the room. She hit her knees and let it all go as he held her hair back. This wasn't the fun Saturday he'd expected to have with her when she'd invited him over last weekend.

She leaned back a few minutes later and looked up at him. Her eyes were red and sweat beaded on her forehead and temples as she whispered, "I don't feel good."

He could imagine that was an understatement. She looked like she could use a do-over. "You think you want to lie down now?"

Her voice was hoarse as she whispered, "Yeah."

Marcus led her to the bedroom she indicated and helped her into bed. Looking around for something that might save the floor if she hurled again, he grabbed a small waste bin from the adjoining bathroom and set it beside her bed.

Tori was curled on her side, staring at the wall, when he asked, "Are you gonna be okay?"

A tear crawled over the bridge of her nose as she said, "My ex-husband called me today."

Marcus stood paralyzed beside her bed. Tori had been married? The news was a punch to the gut.

"He wanted to tell me he's getting married, and he didn't want me to find out from someone else."

He couldn't stand the pain in her voice as her shoulder shook and her chin quivered, so he sat on the bed beside her and rubbed a hand up and down her arm.

"I don't even think I loved him, but he didn't want me anyway. He wanted someone else." Her shaky words were almost too quiet to hear. "And then you left me too."

"I didn't leave you." *Was that how she saw it?*

"You did. You left before I had a chance to see if I'm the problem." Tori turned her face to the pillow and shook as she cried.

How could he have misinterpreted things with her so badly? His chest ached, and her sobs felt like the deepest punishment for his insensitivity.

Marcus pulled her to him and held her close as she cried on his chest. She cried hard and loud, letting her frustrations out while the alcohol swam in her blood.

He'd wanted to hold her, but not like this. This was painful and left him feeling like dirt. He wanted her happy and taking witty jabs at him for being a jerk, but he also wanted her holding him, kissing him, and caring for him the way he cared about her.

He let her cry it out, and when her tears stopped, he felt her relax in his arms, but he couldn't let her go. When her breathing evened out and he knew she was sound asleep, he laid her down on the pillow and tucked her back in.

Marcus pulled an old rocking chair beside the bed and watched her for a while to make sure she would stay asleep. He'd never seen anyone so heartbroken and vulnerable. It was a stark contrast to the unemotional façade she wore. He didn't know what any of this would mean in the morning, but tonight, he was happy to be here for her.

He'd always been able to read people. He knew their true intentions, their mannerisms, their personality quirks, and their tendencies, but Tori was the exception to every rule. Looking at her in the dim moonlight shining through the window, he wondered if he'd ever be able to figure out a creature as complex as Victoria Sanders.

CHAPTER TWELVE

Tori

Tori woke to blinding sunlight streaming through the window and a splitting headache to match her embarrassment.

What had she done? Unfortunately, she remembered something about her divorce and calling Marcus names before vomiting and crying. A part of her hoped she never had to face him again, and her chest tightened at the thought of that loss.

She pushed herself from the bed and shuffled to the kitchen. A pot of coffee was the first thing on her list, so she chugged a bottle of water while the drink that would forever be her strongest choice brewed.

She'd left every curtain open yesterday before storming out to drink her sorrows away, and the blinding sun was more than she could stand at this hour. Looking out the picture window in the kitchen at the peaceful river left her feeling wretched.

Marcus took care of her last night after she was cruel to him, and she wondered if the ache in her chest was possibly the illusive broken heart that people with stronger relationships sometimes talked about.

Marcus had come for her after she'd been snarky to him. He'd been inconvenienced, but he'd showed up when he didn't have to. The conversation she'd had with her mother last week rang in Tori's mind. He'd gone above and beyond for her time and time again.

Birds sang by the river as the gentle breeze moved through the hanging strands of the willow trees on the bank, and she realized she hadn't stopped working on the cabin long enough to look at the beautiful river.

She grabbed her cup of coffee and stepped outside, pulling her sweater tighter around her neck. The swing hanging on the porch reminded her of that first day she'd come to town when Marcus had sat here drenched from carrying her things in through the storm.

Sitting on a front porch swing drinking a cup of coffee sounded like a southern thing to do, but it felt right given the setting. It was something she'd never have done in Chicago, even if she'd had a porch to swing on. Things were just different here. *She* was different here, and it was hard to put a finger on how she felt about the changes. In most ways, she felt better, but this wasn't her real life. It was more of a vacation. A vacation with work and maddening emotions that kept her up at night.

The pity party was really getting started when she heard the rumbling of an engine coming up the drive. The cabin was far enough out of town that she expected visitors to be scarce, but there was one person she wasn't sure she wanted to see headed her way.

Marcus parked the Mustang at the edge of the porch and got out slowly. He didn't speak, but he stopped on the top step.

Tori bit the side of her lip as he leaned on the railing to watch her.

"Can we put our swords away today?" she asked.

He stepped toward her, but when he didn't make a move to sit, she looked out at the river and asked, "Will you walk with me?"

He nodded, and she asked, "You want some coffee?"

At last, he spoke. "No, thanks."

She set her own mug down on the porch beside the swing and wrapped her arms around her middle as they walked toward the riverbank. The trees were almost bare from the early frost and harsh cold that had come on in the last few weeks, and the strings of willow branches hung sad from the thin trunks.

Wetumpka River was wide and constant, and the flow was slow and steady like the town. Life was certainly different here.

They stopped near the bank and stood in silence, taking in the natural wonders of the changing season. She wasn't sure what to say, but her unintended confession of her divorce was a tangible presence between them.

"I'm sorry about last night." She picked at her fingernail as the wind blew her hair in her face. "I was a mess, and I didn't mean to share so much."

Marcus took a step closer to her and ran a hand over his head. "It's okay. We don't have to talk about it."

She turned to him and truly saw him in the morning light. Marcus was possibly the most understanding person she'd ever met, and she was grateful.

He stuck his hand in the pocket of his jeans. "Just please don't make me go there again."

Tori nodded. "Okay."

It was one request, and she'd be glad to make that promise to him and put it behind them because she knew that's what it was now—a part of the past where it would stay.

She closed the last of the space between them and let her hand rest on his forearm. He was warm despite the harsh air, and she moved her hand to slide farther up his arm. She'd never understood the connection people gained from touch before, never felt a rush or sensation from the contact of skin next to skin the way she felt now with Marcus, and his shirt and jacket were barriers between them.

Her fingertips ignited, sending a jolt of warmth through her body. How could something so small be so powerful?

She looked up into his eyes and saw the hurt there. She'd caused him more pain than she realized last night, and she was angry with herself for what she'd done.

"I'm sorry." The words were a whisper on the wind, but she knew he'd heard her when he wrapped her in his arms and pulled her close.

Her own arms locked around him, and she clung to him tight. The things between them—the trust, the honesty, the acceptance—was something she'd never known before.

Their relationship was a series of hot and cold. One minute their sharp tongues squared off, while the next she wanted to be here, wrapped in his arms. In the cold morning, with all her senses, she couldn't deny there was something between them worth protecting, but how far would it get them?

Marcus leaned his cheek to rest on top of her head. "Did you really read about the verse?"

"I did, but I didn't understand it like you said I would." It was a far step out of her comfort zone to admit her ignorance, but she felt comfortable with Marcus in a way she hadn't with anyone before.

"You're not meant to, yet." He rubbed her back and sighed. "But maybe soon I can tell you. I just can't yet. Can you be patient with me?"

She realized he still hadn't told her anything about his life, other than he owned an auto repair shop. Her accusation that he was married rang in her mind, but she pushed it aside. She trusted his words when he'd told her he wasn't married that night.

A war raged inside her as she thought of her mother's advice to give people a chance. Her instinct to push him away for his secrecy was strong, but she hadn't trusted him with the whole truth about herself either. She'd let slip a small piece about her divorce last night, and he'd respected her wishes to let the information lie sleeping between them for now.

"I can wait."

They stood in silence wrapped together against the cold wind, and she thought about what would come next for her. She didn't know what she was looking for, and if she went back home to Chicago as she'd intended, where would that leave this fragile relationship she'd been thrown into with the mysterious man in her arms?

"Do you believe in God, Tori?" The words were quiet enough to meld into the peaceful silence they'd created.

She thought for a moment before answering, "Yeah, I do. I just don't know anything beyond that."

Marcus ran a calloused hand over her hair and nodded his acceptance of her confession.

"I'm a nurse. I see the perfect way our bodies work, and I can't help but think something truly amazing made us that way. I just don't know who or why."

She settled closer into his embrace and sighed. "I read about how God created the world the other night, and I had the feeling that I've seen that great power before in the healing that goes on in the hospital. I've listened and held hands with patients and their families while they prayed, but I don't know how it works. I just know I've seen it happen."

When she paused, he didn't prod her or fill the silence, so she continued. "We've come so far from what God intended us to be. People, I mean."

Marcus pushed her shoulders back so he could look her in the eyes. "Do you want to go to church with me this morning?" he asked.

It was Sunday morning, and she hadn't thought a thing about attending a service since she was a child. "I'm still hungover."

He rubbed her shoulders and gave her that crooked smile she adored. "If they let me in, they'll let you in too, angel."

"Could I take you up on it for next week?" Was she really making plans as if their tumultuous relationship would still be standing then?

"Next week it is."

She took his hand and they walked leisurely back toward the cabin. From this view by the river, the house was beautiful set against the dying forest behind it.

"Can I see you before Sunday?" she asked when they were close to the cabin.

Marcus squeezed her hand. "If you want to."

"I do." For the first time in as long as she could remember, she wanted something more than work and the crash from exhaustion that had become her life in Chicago.

Tori had felt fulfilled before, but things were different here. *She* was different here, and she wanted more.

They stopped at his bright-red Mustang that stood out against the natural scene around them, and he said, "I'll call you tomorrow and we can work it out."

As she watched him drive down the gravel drive, she knew he would call tomorrow like he'd said he would. Her mother was right about her problems trusting others. The issue was hers, not theirs, and it wasn't fair to hold others accountable for her fear of being let down.

Her phone rang in her back pocket as she turned to go inside. Checking it as she walked up the porch steps, her heart sank when she saw it was Scott.

She could let it go to voicemail, but that would be running, and she didn't want to be afraid anymore. He couldn't hurt her more than he already had when he'd cheated on her and divorced her.

"Hello."

"Victoria, where are you?" Scott almost sounded frantic.

"I'm at the cabin in Georgia. Why?"

"What are you doing there?"

"Well, it's really none of your concern, but since this is the only residence I had to my name after you left me, I decided to come down here and get it ready to sell."

"You're selling it?" His outrage was unexpected.

"I can't really keep it, and if I'm going to find a place of my own, I need the money."

"It's just—" He huffed loudly and continued. "I didn't want you to sell it. I thought you'd just leave it and forget about it."

"But I didn't have anywhere else to go. I've been staying with my mom, but she lives too far from the hospital. I've got to find someplace closer." She wondered why he'd called in the first place. "Wait, why did you want to know where I am?"

"A friend called me last night and said there was a woman in a bar in Georgia talking about her house on the river. He realized it was my house and called to let me know."

"It's not your house anymore, and how do you know people in Carson?"

"The question is, how do *you* know people in Carson? He said you left with Marcus Channing last night. What exactly were you thinking?"

She stood paralyzed as the air in her lungs turned to lead. "How do you know Marcus?"

"It doesn't matter."

"You're right. It doesn't because we're divorced, and I don't owe you an explanation." She tried to remember if she'd told Marcus Scott's name last night. If Marcus knew her ex-husband, she might have a more harmful secret than she realized.

Or maybe *his* secrets were worse than she'd feared.

"You're getting married, Scott. Stop calling me. What I'm doing isn't any of your concern anymore."

"I knew I would regret conceding that cabin to you." His tone was sharp and hateful, and it took her by surprise.

She schooled her voice and said, "You owed this cabin to me and so much more. You owed me a lifetime of faithfulness! You tore our marriage apart."

"Don't act like it was something to be treasured," he spat at her.

"Vows and loyalty mean nothing to you."

Tori had never truly loved Scott, but she'd respected him until he'd broken her trust and turned her life into a lie. She would have lived the rest of her life with him. Now, she could see the mess her life had been with him, and she knew they were better off apart.

"Don't sell the house." It sounded like he was giving her an order.

"I have to, Scott."

He ended the call without a good-bye, and she laid the phone on the kitchen island in shock. How could Scott be angry with her when she was just trying to get her life back? The injustice was like being kicked while she was down.

She looked out the window and regretted her decision not to go to church with Marcus this morning. There was still time to catch him, but her mood was sinking lower by the minute.

Instead of calling one man to pick her up after another man hurt her, she decided to drown herself in the never-ending list of chores she needed to do before she could list the cabin on the market.

Chapter Thirteen

Tori

Tori had seen Marcus in brief moments of stolen time during the last week, and she knew while her schedule was lax right now, his wasn't. He worked long hours at the shop, but not as long as she'd worked as a nurse, and he often had some obligation he needed to see to afterward.

He was always apologetic, and she could tell he was concerned about the lack of time he had to spend with her, but she'd told him she would be patient until he was ready to tell her more about himself. She still hadn't mustered the courage to ask him how he knew Scott Wright, and she would be the first to admit she was scared to bring it up.

By Thursday night, she'd been able to get satellite television installed in the cabin, and she'd heard all about the coming storm. The weather report was clear that it should be nothing more than thunder and heavy rain with possible flash flooding in places, but that didn't diminish her concerns.

Marcus had mentioned earlier in the week that they didn't see too many destructive storms in Carson, except in the changing of the seasons, such as now. They were far enough north in Georgia to be partially protected by the foothills of the Appalachian Mountains, but she'd watched the sky grow heavier over the last few days, and her childlike fear was mounting. It was barely 5:00 PM, but the sky was as dark as night and the wind whistled through the trees.

Tori had given up on pruning the shrubs an hour earlier when the clouds began rolling above her. It had only now begun to rain, but her anxiety had been mounting for hours. Now, she was pacing around the couch in the living room wondering who thought a floor-to-ceiling bay window in the main room was a good idea when designing this house.

She made a pot of coffee to distract her mind from the growing storm outside and help keep her alert for as long as it might last. There wasn't a chance she'd be sleeping tonight, unless the storm passed.

Tori sat glued to the emergency weather report that played on three different local stations for the next hour, until the satellite connection was lost. Sitting up straighter, the cadence of her heart hit an all-time high as she wondered how she could track the storm. Following those polygons across the map was pivotal during weather like this.

Reaching for her phone like a lifeline, she called Marcus. Maybe he could talk her down from the panic she felt rising.

He answered on the second ring. "Hey, angel. Don't worry. I'm almost there."

Stunned, she thought she'd misheard. "What?"

"I'm on my way. I didn't want you to be alone during the storm."

Tori hadn't meant to ask him to come, though she'd desperately wanted to, but he'd come running to save her on his own. It was such a selfless and considerate thing to do.

"Okay. Please be careful."

When he arrived three minutes later, she stood in the doorway and watched him run through the pouring rain from his car. Once on the porch, he took quiet, cautious steps toward her like a mountain lion prowling the night.

He didn't say anything as he stepped up to her, and she took his hand to lead him inside. She shut the door behind them and instantly felt the comfort of his presence and the sealed exit settle around her.

As soon as they were inside, Marcus pulled her into his arms and held her. He couldn't protect her from the storm, but the weather wasn't actually out to get her tonight. It was her own insecurities, and she was glad he'd seen enough of her in a few short weeks to know she needed him beside her.

She'd never opened up to Scott about her fear of storms, and she hadn't needed to with Marcus. He just knew, and she was thankful for his uncanny gift for observation and discernment.

Tori hadn't ever asked for Scott's comfort during a storm, and she barely knew the mysterious man who held her tonight. So much was still left to be confessed between them. Marcus was all jagged edges, while Scott had been as smooth and predictable as glass. It didn't make sense why she felt that trusting Marcus was as natural as trusting her own mother.

Actually, maybe it did make sense. Marcus had come running for her before she'd even asked. He saw her need before she had. He'd been thinking of her before she'd thought of him. He ran out into a storm because she was scared.

"I'm sorry," she whispered against his chest as his arms wound tight around her.

"Don't be." He kissed the top of her head just as the electricity flickered and went out.

She leaned back out of his embrace and he chuckled.

"What's so funny?" she asked.

"I'm just thinking about how you would have squealed if you'd been alone when the lights went out."

Tori wrinkled her nose and swatted his arm. "Stop it. I don't know where the candles or flashlights are, so make yourself useful and help me look for them."

Using the flashlights on their phones, they were able to locate five candles and two flashlights, along with some old matches in a drawer in the laundry room. They lit the emergency stash of candles and placed them in a line on the coffee table before settling in on the couch. Marcus sat on one end and tugged on her hand to direct her to sit beside him where she curled against him.

The wind howled and shook the house, while thunder boomed and lightning flashed. The storm was out there, raging and unstoppable, but she was inside, tucked close to the man who wasn't fazed by the weather or her irrational fear.

"Talk to me, please?" she whispered into the dark room.

He didn't speak at first, and she wondered if he'd heard her over the raging storm. He massaged the back of her hand with his thumb, and said, "I didn't expect you."

Tori chuckled. She knew what he meant. "I would say the same, but I did call you for help that day." A lot had changed between them in two and a half weeks. "I think I knew then you'd always come for me."

He hugged her tighter and laughed deep and sweet. "I'm a glutton for punishment."

She laughed with him and lifted her head from his shoulder to look at him, but his usual dark eyes were surrounded by more shadows. The candlelight flickered around them, and she wondered how she'd gotten here—to this place with this man—and what she'd done to change the course of her life so drastically.

Marcus placed a calloused hand on her cheek and rubbed small circles there with his thumb. She couldn't breathe as he whispered, "We're so different."

Tori knew what he meant. His rough hands were a stark contrast to her smooth skin, but she also knew he was wrong. "No. We're the same in the ways that matter. Can't you see that?"

There was one way they were different that would matter to him, and that was her faith. While she wasn't where she wanted to be yet, she was trying to prove to him she was eager to learn more. He'd made a point to invite her to church with him, and she would be there, trying her best to understand.

His brows drew together, and he whispered, "I want to." He shook his head and sighed. "But I'm not a doctor, Tori. I'm a mechanic."

The darkness around her seemed to pool inside her middle, strangling the breath from her lungs. "How did you know about Scott?"

"When you said you were divorced, I put two and two together, since you're living in the house he grew up in. He must have messed up bad to let go of this house. It's been in the Wright family for generations."

Tori looked at him as if she'd never laid eyes on him before. How had she not known where Scott grew up? They'd been married for years, and it never came up. No wonder he didn't want her to sell the house.

"He cheated on me. Then he left me… for her." There it was again, that ambiguous *her* that didn't have a face or a proper name.

Marcus tilted his head and pushed his hand over her cheek and through her hair. "I'm sorry."

She shook her head. "I'm not anymore."

His hand resting on the back of her head pulled her closer until their lips were a breath apart, but he only lingered for a second. His mouth sealed with hers, and she wrapped her arms around his neck.

Tori sucked in a breath and relaxed into his embrace. Marcus' rough, bad boy looks were a complete disguise for the passionate man inside. His kiss was cherishing, cleansing, and she knew in her heart he felt the same awakening that she felt. Something changed when her soul decided it had found someone else to speak to, to reach for, and she would never be the same.

Tori never meant to get attached to someone, not even her ex-husband, but it was impossible to fight the recognition of herself that she saw in Marcus.

When he pulled away, his sly grin reflected that playful side she'd come to adore. "The storm's over, angel."

She looked around and the silence hit her. Even the rain had receded to nothing but a mist, and she hadn't noticed. He'd pulled her attention from the big, bad monster, and she couldn't help but smile. "You're right."

Turning back to him, she asked, "Would you like to stay a little longer?" She wasn't ready to let go of the moment they'd shared, but she certainly wasn't ready for anything else that "staying longer" might imply.

Thinking she should make her invitation clearer, she stammered, "I mean, not for… anything else…" She gestured back and forth between them, unsure of how to just come out and say that she wasn't implying she wanted to sleep with him.

He nodded. "I know. I understand, but I really need to get going." He leaned forward and rested his elbow on his knee while he rubbed a hand over his face.

Marcus sighed and said, "I need to tell you something. If we're gonna keep seeing each other, you need to know."

Her heart sank as she waited for the blow. This was the secret he hadn't been ready to tell her, and it sounded like a big one.

"I have three brothers and a sister… and they live with me." He gestured with his hands while he was talking, and she'd never seen him do that before. It was possible he was just as nervous as she was right now.

"Our mom is addicted to drugs and alcohol, and she neglected all of us at one point or another. When I was old enough and could afford a place of my own, I took them with me. I filed for legal guardianship for all of them, and she didn't fight me."

He turned to look at her and spoke faster as his hands flew through the air. "You see, I have to make sure they get to school on time, and have a ride home from practice, and eat dinner, and do their homework, and—"

Tori placed a hand on his arm. "Marcus, I understand."

"No, you can't. It's not like I can just date you like normal people do. I can't be away from them for long, and I wouldn't have left them tonight if I hadn't been sure the storm wasn't anything to be worried about. I'm tied to this life I didn't choose, and it's not fair to you."

She shook her head. "Life's not fair, and I know that. Now that I know about your family, I can be understanding of the things you have to do for them. I get it. They *should* come first. Maybe I can help you."

Marcus stood. "No, it's not your burden. Not that I think they're a burden, they're my family. But it's hard sometimes." He brushed a hand over his face and through his short hair. "It's just not easy."

She stood and went to him, taking his hands in hers. "You said that, and I heard you. I know it'll be different, but we can do this. I won't ask you to neglect them like your mom did. I can see that they need you, and I'm thankful they have someone who cares enough to *want* to be there for them."

He didn't say anything. He just stared at her, so she continued. "I want to do this, and this doesn't change things for us."

Marcus looked down at their linked hands. "I guess you're right. I just wish I could give you more."

She smiled. "You've given me so much. I can't believe you charged out into the storm tonight to be with me. You're a good man, Marcus."

He stopped before asking, "You want to go to the fair on Saturday? My brothers and sister will be there too, so it's not exactly a date, but I think you'd like it."

Her eyes opened wide as she asked, "A fair? I've never been to a fair. That sounds like fun." She was really turning this trip to Georgia into a string of firsts.

"I'll pick you up at 6:00 PM. Dress warm. This cold front is no joke." He wasn't exaggerating. The temperatures had been plummeting in the last few days, and she'd had to shop for warmer clothing this week.

"It's a date."

Marcus' smile was glowing in the moonlight shining through the receding clouds. "If you say so." He pulled her close and held her for a quiet moment. "You're the most interesting and unexpected woman I've ever met."

"I'll take that as a compliment."

He chuckled and kissed the top of her head before she led him to the door where they said their good-byes.

He kissed her again on the porch, and she lifted onto her toes trying to get closer to him. No, he was the interesting one. Marcus had no idea how thoroughly he'd changed her life.

Chapter Fourteen

Marcus

Marcus had been a nervous wreck all day, and the only way to hide it was to be ten times quieter than usual. If he opened his mouth, someone would figure it out.

Tori agreed to go to the fair with him, but that also meant introducing her to his family. It was soon—too soon if you asked him—but she already knew about them. Any efforts he made to keep the people in his life away from each other was more trouble than it was worth.

What if she didn't like them? Or if they didn't like her? It frustrated him that something he had no control over could dictate his future with Tori. There wasn't anything to do now except wait and see what would happen.

He'd conceded that Brandon could drive the younger kids to the fair in his Mustang, even if it killed Marcus to do it. There were just enough seats in the car for the kids, but they wouldn't all fit with Tori. Plus, he couldn't wait to see her reaction when she found out about her chariot for the night.

Marcus arrived at Tori's house a few minutes early and watched her run outside when she heard him rumbling up the drive. A huge smile lit her face, and he could tell she was trying to contain it.

"What's that?" she yelled as soon as the engine died.

"Your ride." He slung his leg over the motorcycle and grabbed the helmet he'd strapped to the back.

She stayed quiet with her gaze on him as he walked up the porch steps and held the helmet out between them. When she reached for it, he drew it back out of her reach and said, "First…" before leaning in to place a sweet kiss on her lips.

When he pulled away, her blue eyes were hazy. He was glad to see she'd worn appropriate clothing for their outdoor adventure. Gone were the pantsuits and heels. They'd been traded in for thick sweaters and jeans with sneakers.

"You're early."

"I wanted to see if there was a reward for promptness." Marcus winked, and he almost chuckled when she sighed.

"One kiss," she said, and held up a single finger.

He licked his lips with a grin and took a step toward her. As the thud of his heavy boots on the porch echoed around them in the twilight, she grinned and took a step back to match his own. Two more steps, advancing and retreating, and her back was flush against the closed door.

Marcus stopped when they were mere inches apart and said, "One kiss?"

Tori looked up at him and whispered, "Yeah."

Slow was the game as he leaned down and hovered a mere breath from her lips without touching her. He still held the helmet, and his other hand was wrapped behind his back.

He enjoyed their playful affections, and he knew Tori did too. To her credit, she didn't make a move to end the suspense as he waited, tested, and baited her.

When he couldn't wait any longer, he dipped farther down and placed a slow, deep kiss on the side of her neck just below her jawline. He could feel her pulse quicken, and he knew his own beat a similar rhythm.

He waited for her to say something, but she just stood there with her mouth slightly opened, looking at him as if he'd surprised her. His deep chuckle drifted in the growing darkness, and he marveled at the way she made him feel. He'd worried all day, but now, he was laughing. He couldn't remember the last time he'd felt so carefree.

"Come on, angel." He grabbed her hand and tugged her toward the motorcycle. "It's time to learn to ride."

She followed him to the bike, and said, "It's so typical. The bad boy of Carson rides a motorcycle."

"This bike is special, okay? No bad-mouthing it." He pointed a finger at her in mock reprimand. "It took ten years of repairs, trades, and work hours to get me this bike, and if you must know…" He reached out a hand to help her get seated on the bike behind him. "You're the first person to even sit on it."

"What? You're joking." Her pitch spiked, and he wished he could see her face.

"Only the truth. I'm incredibly protective of this bike, and no one gets on it but me. Fortunately for you and Brandon, the Mustang only holds five, so he's driving the kids, and you get me."

Marcus didn't have to tell her to hold on. She snaked her hands around his waist and leaned her head against his back. Tori was uncharacteristically comfortable on the back of his bike, and he wondered how many rides they'd take together.

The engine roared to life, and Tori laughed behind him as the machine rumbled beneath them.

"It's so loud," she screamed in his ear to be heard over the thundering.

He could feel the vibrations in his bones and knew she must be feeling the rush he felt every time he rode. He couldn't deny the power radiating from the bike, but the control was his.

They parked in an open field next to the fairgrounds. The grass was knee high, and he was thankful again she hadn't tried to wear high heels. He helped her off the bike and kept her hand in his as they stood in line to get tickets. Watching her take in the flashing lights against the dark sky was a sight to behold.

When they reached the ticket window, Tori remarked, "Two dollar entry fee? Looks like I'm a cheap date." She squeezed his arm and he laughed. If she only knew.

Once they stepped through the gate and handed their tickets to the attendant, he sent a text to Megan letting her know they'd arrived. His siblings hadn't gone far, since they didn't have money for the rides yet.

Marcus turned to Tori and rubbed his head. "Okay, I guess I should tell you more about them before you meet them. Brandon is almost eighteen, Taylor and Megan are twins, and they're thirteen, and Trey is ten. They, um—"

The sound of running footsteps drew his attention, and he turned to see Trey sprinting toward him. "Brother! They have animals!"

"Oh, yeah?"

Megan jogged up behind Trey and clarified, "It's a petting zoo, but it's five dollars to get in and three dollars for the food you can give them."

"I get it. Here." He handed Megan two hundred dollar bills. "Remember, part of that is for your brothers, and if you need me, call. Don't let Trey out of your sight, and don't let him bother the animals."

"Okay." Megan was staring at Tori and shifting her weight from side to side.

"Meg, this is Tori. Tori, this is my sister, Megan."

"Hey, nice to meet you," Megan said, extending her hand respectfully.

Tori took the extended hand in hers and smiled. "It's a pleasure to meet you too, Megan."

Marcus grabbed Trey by the shoulder and drew his attention. "Trey, this is Tori. Be nice to her."

Tori laughed, and Trey said, "Hey," with a casual wave.

"Nice to meet you, Trey."

"Thanks, brother." Trey held out a fist and Marcus bumped it with his, which sent Trey running off toward the petting zoo.

Megan waved at Tori as she walked backward in the direction Trey had flown. "Bye, Tori."

Tori waved. "Bye, Megan. I'll see you later."

When he looked back to Tori, her brows were drawn together as she asked, "Brother?"

Marcus nodded as he placed a hand on the small of her back to lead her toward the ticket line for rides. "Yeah, he's always called me brother."

"Is that where you got the name for the garage?"

She was putting the pieces together on her own.

"Yep."

"And that's why you said…" She put a hand on his arm, and he turned back to her. "Am I my brother's keeper?"

"Yeah," was all he said.

"It means sometimes you have to do things in life you don't want to do." She repeated his words from the first time they'd met, and he felt too exposed.

"Yeah." They were moving up in line, but there were still a few people ahead of them.

"But you like taking care of your siblings. I can tell."

"I do. I just wish things were different and they didn't have to settle for what I can be for them. I wish they had a mom *and* a dad. They deserve a good family."

"I'm sorry, Marcus. That's a lot of responsibility." She hadn't asked about their dads yet, and he was grateful.

"Megan is the only girl? In a house full of boys?"

Marcus sighed. "Unfortunately. It's hard for her. I can tell. She needs a woman in her life, especially now because she's super hormonal, and I don't know what I'm doing." He tensed when he realized she might interpret his words to mean he was hoping *she* would be that woman.

"I'm sure you're doing okay."

"No, she tells me I'm clueless often enough that I get the hint."

When it was their turn, they opted for the twenty dollar armbands that offered unlimited rides, and Tori cut her eyes to him before looking away. "This is *not* the cheap date I said it was."

He laughed. "No, the kids can blow through a few hundred dollars in a couple of hours here. That's why I started them off with two. If Megan is in charge of the money, it might not be so bad."

They played a few booth games and Marcus won a few prizes Tori had been eying before they met up with Lindsey and Dakota. Jake and Natalie, still newly engaged and smiling, were right behind them. The women hugged Tori, and Marcus felt a weight lifted off his shoulders. Tori fit in with his friends better than he did.

As Tori walked off ahead of him, arms linked with Lindsey and Natalie, he wondered how many weekend nights they could spend with his friends and family doing things like this, learning each other, having fun, and living this happy life.

Dakota slapped Marcus' back as they turned to follow the women toward the Ferris Wheel, the highlight of the night. Tori laughed, her hair flowing in the wind, and Lindsey yelled over her shoulder, "It's the winds of change, folks!"

Marcus looked up just as the rain hit his face and thunder rumbled in the distance. They were only expecting light rain tonight, but his concern grew as he looked to Tori, worried she'd be afraid to be out in the open.

Tori looked back at him over her shoulder, and her smile was nothing short of gorgeous. She didn't care about the rain or the lingering thunder. Tori was headed for the Ferris Wheel, and he'd follow her anywhere.

CHAPTER FIFTEEN

Marcus

Sunday came, and so did Marcus' anxiety. He'd asked Tori to come to church with him, and she'd agreed. Why was he still nervous? She could still back out, and that was the fear that had been chasing him for a week.

Megan stormed into the kitchen and propped her hand on her hip. "Marcus, Trey won't get out of my room so I can get dressed."

"Trey, get out of her room!" Marcus yelled down the hallway as he pushed the scrambled eggs onto a plate. "Get dressed quick. The eggs are ready."

Megan rolled her eyes and stormed back to her room. Trey and Taylor came barreling into the dining room and sent chairs skidding across the laminate floor as they flopped into their seats.

Taylor shoved a forkful of eggs into his mouth as soon as they'd said grace. "Hey, can I go home from church with Bentley? His mom said she would take us to the batting cages today."

One less sibling to entertain sounded like a good idea. "Sure. I'll talk to his mom after the service."

Brandon joined them in silence and the four boys ate breakfast with no sign of Megan. Marcus stood from the table and ordered the boys to clean up before he knocked on Meg's door.

He couldn't give Megan much, but he'd worked hard to be able to afford a house big enough for her to have her own space. Unfortunately, that meant Taylor and Trey were still roommates, and they might drive him crazy soon. He'd rather sleep on the couch than suffer through too much more of their bickering.

"Meg, what's wrong?"

Her muffled voice was distorted through the door between them. "Just go away. I'm not hungry."

Marcus let his forehead rest on the cold wood of the door. "You know you can talk to me. I'm not good at talking back, but I can listen."

He heard a sniffle on the other side of the door and hated his uselessness. "What can I do, Meg?"

"Nothing. I'll be out in a little bit."

True to her word, Meg emerged from her room red faced and teary eyed just in time to get in the car. Megan was his only sister, and he had a soft spot for her that was matched only by Trey. Megan was an outcast, but he'd seen Trey endure more than any child should have to since their mom was much worse off by the time he came around, and it was Marcus' mission in life to make up for the unseen scars their mother's neglect had caused.

The ride to church was tense. Meg was silent, staring out the window, while Taylor and Trey annoyed each other. Brandon typed furiously on his phone the entire ride, but Marcus couldn't complain. If Brandon wasn't distracted by his phone or football, he was a handful.

Tori's Mercedes wasn't in the parking lot when they arrived, and he tried to keep his thoughts on herding the kids into the church without someone running off and getting into trouble. Taylor had already asked to sit with Bentley, but the answer was no. It would always be no, as long as Marcus needed to be within arm's length of his brother in case he decided to chat during the service. Marcus wasn't above swatting Taylor's head in front of the congregation if the need arose.

When they reached the door, Marcus hung back to wait for Tori, and Meg stood with him. He knew she had something to say, but he couldn't read her mind for love nor money.

Meg stood beside him with her arms crossed over her middle, watching the people mill about. At last, she turned to him and whispered. "Can I sit with Macy?"

He didn't have a problem with that. Meg could be trusted to sit with her friends during the church service and not cause a stir, but just as he opened his mouth to tell her to go on, she stopped him.

"Never mind, Tori's here."

He turned around to see Tori walking up with a smile on her face wearing her Chicago sleek clothing and looking like a corporate Barbie doll.

"Hey, sorry I couldn't get here sooner. I drove slow because I'm not familiar with the roads yet." Tori turned to Megan with a smile. "Good morning, Megan. I love that dress."

Meg let her arms fall to her sides and sighed. "Thanks, I couldn't find any shoes to wear with it this morning."

Tori looked down at the black and white Converse shoes Meg was wearing and laughed. "I think you did just fine. It's good to have your own style, but I have some wedges that would look amazing with that dress. What size do you wear?"

"Seven."

Tori snapped her fingers and held her hands out, palms up, as if she'd solved a problem. "Perfect. Looks like we can share shoes." Tori gasped. "And we can shop together! I need to update my winter wardrobe. Somehow it seems colder here than in Chicago."

Megan's smile was brighter than he'd ever seen it. "Are you kidding? We can go shopping?"

Tori turned to Marcus and asked, "When can we take a girl's day and update our wardrobes?"

He was at a loss for words. Tori just walked in and knew what was wrong with Meg. How could he have known Megan was crying about her shoes, of all things? "Um, any day."

Megan bounced on her toes beside him. "Can she pick me up from school on Tuesday? It's a review day for the exam, but I took it early, so I don't need it. Please."

Marcus was incredibly proud of Megan for acing all of her college prep classes and taking her midterm exams early, but he never let the kids leave school early. This time, it seemed like it would do more good than harm.

"I think that'll work." He turned to Tori and grabbed her hand. "Are you okay with picking her up from school?"

"Of course! I'm excited. Shopping is one of my favorite things to do."

Megan grabbed Tori's other hand and asked, "Can I sit by you?"

"I'd love that. I don't know anyone, and it's been a long time since I've been to church."

Megan's eyes opened wide, and she tugged Tori into the church. "Come on. I'll introduce you to people."

Marcus let Megan drag her around only because he saw that it made Tori comfortable to be with someone who was brimming with joy to see her. He'd worried his family wouldn't like her, but they seemed to be getting along well.

Brandon stepped up beside him, phone in hand, and asked, "Who's that with Megan?"

Marcus frowned and took the phone from his brother. It was one of his church rules. There were only two, really. No talking during service, and no phones in church.

"That's Tori, my girlfriend."

Brandon's dark eyes that were so much like his own widened in shock. "No way. That's your girlfriend? Since when do girls give you the time of day?"

"I *could* have a life, you know? You're just too absorbed in your phone to notice."

"But she's hot." Brandon pointed at Tori, who was shaking hands with Sissy's mom, Barbara.

Marcus grabbed the back of his brother's neck and leaned in close. "She's out of your league. Plus, she could be your sister-in-law one day."

That was a crazy thought. What if he and Tori *did* get married one day? He didn't see himself as the marrying type, and she'd been down that road once before. Would she want to try it again?

Brandon threw his head back. "Not another sister. That's the last thing I need. Meg is driving me nuts with her crying and screaming fits."

Marcus laughed as he left his brother to join Meg and Tori. He couldn't blame Meg for her outbursts most of the time. Their brothers were a pain in the neck on a good day.

Their pew was full by the time the service began. Trey and Taylor were on his left and Tori and Meg sat to his right. The girls whispered with their heads leaned in close, while Megan shared her Bible with Tori.

Marcus wondered again why Tori was the one person he couldn't read. It was frustrating, but wouldn't it be boring if he always knew what she was thinking? Maybe that's why God had led him to the one he would need to spend his entire life trying to understand.

Brandon sat on the far end of the row behind them and kept eying Tori. Marcus kinda felt sorry for his brother. He was about to turn eighteen, and girls and football were definitely on the brain. He needed to keep Brandon a safe distance from Tori for a while. His brother was right, Tori was hot. Marcus just didn't want Brandon thinking of her that way.

Marcus kept an eye on Tori during the service. He wanted to make sure she felt comfortable here, but so far, she'd given him no indication that she wasn't open to hearing about Christ.

Tori sat absorbed in the sermon. She read the passages and listened intently to every word. Marcus would've given his left arm to know what was going through her head. Church and the Christian way of life was important to him and his family. He'd worked hard to raise the kids in a godly home, and he would be the first to admit that he leaned on God's word often for decision-making and guidance, especially with the kids.

Jesus was his Savior, and he wanted Tori to know what God had done in his life and what He could do in her life too, should she decide to accept Him.

Marcus was quiet, but he treated others the way he wanted to be treated, and that's what he expected in return. He wasn't one to judge someone for who they were, even the city girl beside him. So what if she was from Chicago and had more money than he'd seen in his lifetime? She was the Tori he knew and loved, and that was all that mattered.

Loved? Did he love her? There hadn't been enough time for that, right?

Something settled inside him, and he realized he did.

Love brought with it a multitude of complications. What if she didn't feel the same way? What if she went back to Chicago? She hadn't mentioned it in a while, but she was still doing repairs on the house. What if she didn't want this life? This was all he had to give.

He looked at her, blonde hair shining in the midday light coming through the stained-glass window, and thought he would be incredibly fortunate if he were to be loved by Tori Sanders.

After the service, there was an invitation, a calling for all who wanted to accept Jesus as their Lord and Savior to come and be saved.

The invitation hadn't struck him as a vital part of the service in a while. He'd been saved years ago, as had his siblings, but Tori…

Wrinkles sat above her sandy blonde brows as she listened to the song, and he knew it was too soon to expect her to be able to make a decision. Still, he silently prayed for God to move in her life. He asked God to show him how to lead her in the right direction.

Without thinking about his choice of words, he prayed, *Lord, please bring her home.*

CHAPTER SIXTEEN

Tori

Tori's thoughts were jumbled after the sermon. She had no idea there was so much to learn about Christianity. She was ashamed to admit she'd always thought Christianity was as simple as accepting that God was the Creator and all-powerful and living a life of good deeds.

Oh, had she been wrong. It turned out, trying to be a good person, or what she learned today was following in the footsteps of Jesus, was only one part, and not the most important.

Along with believing that Jesus was the Son of God and that He'd sacrificed himself to seal the salvation of everyone, there was praying and repentance and asking Christ into your heart and soul as your Lord and Savior.

To say her thoughts were merely jumbled was an understatement. Listening to the sermon today felt much like those countless hours she'd spent in nursing school.

She had a lot to learn, but the challenge felt good. Tori had always loved school and learning. She had a master's degree, and she'd contemplated a doctorate. Of course, all her academic years hadn't prepared her for this kind of learning. She'd have to talk to Marcus about how to move forward.

She was used to critical thinking and situational testing, but learning about Christianity would require emotional growth as well. Connections with people were hard for her, but would it be the same with Christ?

Surprisingly, after the sermon, she realized she felt closer to Marcus and understood him better. Not just because he'd sat with her and reached for her hand during prayer. She felt… stronger with him near, and she knew she'd be better with him standing beside her.

Megan ran up to her as they made their way outside. "Hey, can you come over and help me figure out what to wear to school this week?"

"Sure…" She realized that Marcus hadn't invited her over yet, and she was sure he had a reason. She respected his decision to keep his family private, but now that she'd met most of them, she wasn't sure why he hadn't extended an invitation.

"Actually, we might need to ask Marcus first." Tori thought it was better to be safe than sorry.

Marcus walked up behind her and placed a hand on the small of her back. "You want to grab some lunch? We usually go to The Line after church."

"That sounds great. I haven't been there before, but—"

"Can Tori help me pick out clothes to wear to school next week?" Megan interrupted.

Marcus stammered, "Um, you mean shopping?"

"No, from my closet. Can she come over after lunch?"

Marcus hesitated before nodding. "Sure. That sounds great. Since Taylor is spending the day with a friend, we have room in my car if you'd like to ride with us."

Megan piped up. "Can I just ride with Tori?"

Tori smiled and turned to Marcus. "We can just follow you in my car." She was thrilled that Megan wanted to spend time with her. She liked the girl, and it was nice to spend time with someone new.

"Okay, we'll see you there. Meg knows the way, in case we get split up." He leaned in and kissed Tori's cheek before herding the boys into the Mustang.

Megan was a ball of energy during the short drive to The Line. They talked about her outfit ideas and had just touched on the broad topic of makeup when they arrived at the restaurant.

Megan stepped from the car with a genuine grin that looked just like Marcus'. Their charming smile was one shared trait they couldn't deny. The same could be said for their chocolate hair. While Marcus' hair was cut short, his sister's hung straight down her back.

Lunch was full of surprises. Trey and Taylor didn't stop talking, and Megan and Marcus sat quietly. Marcus' silence made sense now.

When her brothers would taunt her, Megan just rolled her eyes and went back to eating. It was a good thing she didn't let the little things get to her. Marcus was probably a good role model for patience.

Tori watched with a smile as Marcus quietly paid for her lunch and opened the door for her on the way out as if it were second nature. She was an independent woman, but it was sweet to see Marcus doing little things for her when he didn't have to. Every minute he spent with her was a gift, and she understood that now that she'd met his family. The boys alone were exhausting.

Meg was probably difficult for Marcus to understand. The young teenager had latched onto Tori like a lifeline, and Meg wouldn't dream of letting go. Tori saw the need Meg had for a woman in her life, and she was happy to be there for her.

Meg talked Tori's ears off all the way to Marcus' house after lunch, stopping every now and then to tell her where to turn.

Tori wanted Marcus to share this part of his life with her, but she didn't want to force him into it like this. If only she'd had time to talk to him about it before she'd said she would come today.

Tori drove down a quiet country road Meg had pointed out and wondered if he'd be upset about being forced into this decision. She was trying to listen to Meg's questions about concealer, but she was worried about Marcus.

After a minute of driving, Meg pointed out a driveway that led to a square house on a low rise not far off the road. The precursor to winter had been unseasonably cold this year, and the trees and grass around the house were a lifeless brown. With unobtrusive beige walls and faded brown shutters, the place almost blended into the winter landscape. A small shed sat behind the house nestled against the dying tree line.

Marcus met Tori at her car when she stepped out. "Hey, Meg, can you give us a minute?"

His sister waved them off and ran toward the house.

Tori couldn't read his expression as he gestured to the house like Vanna White presenting letters on *Wheel of Fortune*. "I should have warned you not to expect much."

"Marcus, I want you to share your life with me, but if you're not ready, I can come back some other time."

"No, I really want you to be here. I just wish I had more to show you. This is it."

"And this is perfect. Can I get a tour?"

He laughed and began pointing at the entryway. "As you can see, we opt for shrubbery around here. Flowers are too needy, and the boys would kill them on purpose."

She laughed. "I bet you don't have time for flowers. Actually, I wish you could have seen my loft in Chicago. It was… lifeless. There wasn't anything extra or lively in the entire place.

So, don't feel bad that you don't have pretty flowers to greet your guests. I get it. I spent my life working and not enough time thinking about how to really live my life." Looking at the life she was living with Marcus now, it sounded like something she should cultivate.

He nodded his understanding as he opened the door for her to enter. A brown stained porch ran along the front of the house that matched the tin roof. The inside was clean and as unadorned as the exterior.

"I didn't know we'd be having an important visitor today. Sorry it's not nice."

Tori turned to him. "Don't you see? It doesn't matter what your house looks like. Everything about you is becoming very important to me. Everything you show me is a part of you I didn't know before. It feels like I'm being let into your life." She whispered, "And you know how important that is to me."

He pulled her to him and into a crushing hug. "I'm sorry. I know you won't think less of me because of where I live."

"It's the opposite. I can't believe you've done so much and cared for your brothers and sister at the same time. I'm proud of you. Your siblings are doing remarkably well for having a broody, bad boy mechanic for a guardian."

They both laughed, and he pulled out of the hug but grabbed her hand. "I'll show you to Meg's room."

CHAPTER SEVENTEEN

Marcus

Things were almost too good to be true. Megan was doing better since Tori came around, Brandon was reaching the end of football season, and Marcus' relationship with Tori had only grown over the last few days.

He wasn't used to things going right in his life. Undoubtedly, he'd find out soon that Trey had pranked a teacher at school or Taylor had gotten detention, but for now, things were better than ever.

It was crazy to sit around expecting the sky to fall, but Marcus couldn't help wondering when it would all crumble. Tori was the new factor here, and they'd come off the starting line gunning from zero to sixty in no time. He was falling, or had already fallen, and there had to be a point when the emotional uplift stopped.

What did she even see in him? He couldn't give her enough of his time, he didn't have a fraction of the money she was used to, and he wasn't some romantic heartthrob that women fawned over.

The looming threat was that she would move on like she was supposed to, and he'd be left here, feeling different and lonelier than he was before knowing her. Losing her now would be hard. He loved her. How had he allowed that to happen?

He wiped his sweaty palms on the greasy rag in his pocket just as Meg came running in the side entrance to the auto shop. "Marcus, we bought some of the cutest clothes today! Thanks for letting me go."

His sister stopped short of the hug she'd intended when she noticed his filthy uniform. "Ew, you're gross."

Tori walked into the shop behind Megan and the sight of his girlfriend felt like a kick in the chest. She was always a welcome vision after the days he spent turning wrenches and paying bills.

He turned back to Meg. "You got homework?"

"No, but I want to call Abby and tell her about my new clothes."

He pointed toward the waiting room. "Go. I'll come get you when it's time to leave."

Meg ran off and thanked Tori on her way out.

"How'd it go?" Marcus asked Tori as he stepped closer and placed a sweet kiss on her cheek, careful not to touch her anywhere else and smear grease.

"Great. We had fun and got her some really cute stuff. She's set for the season."

"What about you? Anything new?"

"Actually, I found one of those flannel jackets like you wear all the time. Why didn't you tell me the secret to staying warm is fleece and flannel?"

He laughed and guided her into the office. "I can't wait to see you in flannel."

"I'll have you know it's fashionable here. All the women are wearing it."

Marcus couldn't remember why he'd been so worried before. His world was on fire when Tori came around, and she made him happy. Meg was stuck to her side, and Tori was good for his family. He wasn't sure what he would've done had she not taken Meg under her wing.

It was unnerving how Tori could turn his day around with just her presence. What would it be like if things *did* work out between them? It was dangerous to hope, but he desperately wanted to have faith.

He made sure to keep one chair in his office clean for when Tori stopped by, and he directed her to the seat as he took his place behind the computer. He could work and talk at the same time, so she would tell him about her day while he wrapped up orders and payroll.

"We really had a good time shopping. I like Meg. I never had any sisters, and it's nice to have someone to hang out with."

"Why didn't you have siblings? I can't imagine what that would be like."

Tori picked at her fingernails in her lap. "Mom and Dad fought a lot when I was young, before they divorced. It was probably a good thing they didn't try again. They divorced when I was five, and I wouldn't have wished that trouble on any siblings I might've had. I watched my parents fight enough. It wasn't fun."

Maybe Tori understood more about his childhood than he thought.

"I know what you mean. I hated it when my mom fought with her boyfriends. Brandon just kept quiet, but Taylor was a force to be reckoned with. He gets that from me I guess. We both would step up before we let anyone lay a hand on her."

"It sounds like there were a few men in her life."

"Over time, yeah. The twins and Trey have the same dad, and Brandon's dad stuck around for a while. I don't remember my dad, so…" He shrugged. "No harm, no foul."

"Is that really the way you see it?"

"I'm not sure. He could have made things worse, but if he wasn't man enough to stick around, I'm pretty sure things wouldn't have been better. I'll never know."

She shrugged and stood to look at the car posters on the walls. "Did you always know you wanted to be a mechanic?"

Marcus chuckled. "What makes you think I wanted to be a mechanic?"

"Oh, I don't know." Tori turned to him, rolling her eyes. "Maybe because it's written all over your face and these walls. You love this. I've seen you working, and you're at peace when you're tinkering on cars."

"Cars are all I've ever known. It started out as something to keep my mind busy, but I have a knack for it, so it turned into a side gig.

Before I knew it, I'd grown my makeshift business out of the backyard shed.

"Mechanics are second nature for me. There's a problem, and there's a way to fix it. You need a part, or something isn't connected right, or you need some maintenance. Overall, it's simple, but I enjoy a challenge."

"Oh, really? With people or cars?"

"Both, but cars are easier. I don't have to wait for a machine to reveal its secrets. They're usually easy to find. People take more time, and sometimes, like with you, I'm wrong."

Tori chuckled. "When did you start the business?"

Marcus stopped typing to think for a moment. "Let's see. Trey was two, so that would be eight years ago? I was almost twenty years old."

"How did you afford a place like this when you were that young?"

"I got a loan from my friend, Brian's, parents. They didn't charge me interest, and they knew I'd pay back every last dime, even if it killed me. Plus, they knew the only way I could support my brothers and sister would be to do something like this."

Tori smiled and leaned her hip against his desk. She knew the kind of distraction she posed while he was trying to finish up work so they could go to dinner, but he enjoyed her taunts. In her fitted jeans and sophisticated sweaters, she was a picture of elegance. She never wore anything revealing or provocative, and that endeared her to him even more. He was drawn to her more than any woman he'd ever known. Her beauty was kindness and understanding, things he had no right getting close to.

He looked down at his grease-stained uniform and wondered how two mismatched people found themselves so irrevocably connected.

"Sounds like you're worth the investment."

He turned back to the spreadsheet before him, suddenly self-conscious from her compliment. "Yeah, that would be a first. So, tell me, why did you decide to become a nurse?"

She leaned back and propped her arm on the desk as she thought. "Well, it started in high school. I was good at the sciences, and I liked them. I liked anatomy, but I also liked physiology. I understood biology, and I aced chemistry. By my sophomore year, I saw the pattern, and I made a decision.

"When I got into nursing school, I learned that it's much more than the academics. Nursing became a way for me to connect with people, and I hadn't been able to do that before. When my dad left, I distanced myself from everyone, except my mom. She was the one person I could count on, and I didn't want anyone to be able to reject me… to leave me, again."

Marcus' chest tightened. How could her dad have just left her? Didn't he know what he was missing?

"Those people, the patients, they needed me, whether they liked it or not. They wanted me around because I could help make them better, and it felt… nice, to be wanted."

"You *are* wanted, Tori." He reached for her hand and linked his fingers with hers.

Now, it was her turn to look flushed and embarrassed. "So," Tori changed the subject, shaking her head, "what're your plans for Thanksgiving?"

Marcus shrugged. "I don't know."

"It's in two days. How do you not know?"

"Well, I wasn't going to plan anything out of the ordinary."

Tori shook her head again. "No. That's unacceptable. I'll be cooking Thanksgiving dinner at my house, and you're bringing the family."

It wasn't lost on him that she called the cabin *her* house. Did she plan to keep it? "Are you sure? You don't have to do that. At least let me help."

"No, I want to do this. It'll be fun. I never thought I'd be having a big Thanksgiving meal, and I want to do it."

Marcus rubbed the stubble on his chin before offering, "Can I send Meg over early to help?"

Tori's eyes opened wider, and she smiled. "That sounds perfect. Yes, I'll come get her at 8:00 that morning. The rest of you can show up around 11:30."

Marcus smiled and reached for the intercom. "Hey, Meg, get in here."

Releasing the button, he leaned back in his chair with his arms behind his head to wait. "You tell her. She's gonna lose her mind."

Meg stepped in a few seconds later with a wan look on her face. "Marcus, Taylor just called and said he found a note stuffed in Trey's backpack that says he's almost failing science."

Marcus dropped his hands from behind his head. "You're joking. We do homework every night. How is he failing?"

"I don't know. The note says she wants to schedule a parent-teacher conference with you after the Thanksgiving holiday."

Marcus closed his eyes and pinched the bridge of his nose. "Great." More time away from work was just what he needed.

He took a deep breath and changed the subject. "Tori has a surprise for you."

Meg's demeanor perked as she turned to Tori. "What's up?"

"You want to help me make Thanksgiving dinner for the family on Thursday?"

"Yes! And I can show you how I organized my closet this week with all the new clothes we bought."

Tori rubbed her hands together in her excitement. "Actually, dinner is at my house."

"We get to see your house? This is so exciting. I'm so raiding your closet for shoe ideas."

"We'll have all day together. Don't worry." Tori winked at his sister, and Meg rushed to Tori, wrapping her in a rib-crushing hug.

Marcus watched the women embrace, and his heart swelled. Seeing his sister happy was rare, and seeing her bonding with Tori was the best thing he could have hoped for. Tori was changing his life, and he couldn't understand how he'd come to be so fortunate.

CHAPTER EIGHTEEN

Marcus

Getting to Tori's house on time wasn't difficult, considering the boys had been ready since their feet hit the floor. Everyone was anxious to see Tori's house, mostly because the stunning northerner still had a cloud of mystery surrounding her. Brandon couldn't figure out what she saw in Marcus, and Trey always talked about how pretty she always dressed.

Meg had been gone since early morning, and it had been a chore to keep the kids entertained. They were restless since school was out, so he decided to get the party started early when they turned onto her gravel driveway at 11:00 on Thanksgiving morning.

Taylor leaned forward between the seats when the stunning cabin came into view and shouted, "You didn't tell us she lives in the Wright House!"

Brandon put his phone down and looked up. "No way. How'd she snag this place?"

"She lives in a mansion!" Trey yelled.

Marcus just chuckled. "It's not a mansion, but don't break anything, and don't make a mess. Are we clear?"

They all nodded and murmured their acceptance as he parked the car. Marcus herded the boys to the door and knocked before turning around to remind them to behave.

Meg opened the door wearing a smile and a brown apron with white lace around the edges. "Come in. Dinner is almost ready." His sister held the door open and made a grand gesture for them to enter.

The whole family was enchanted with Tori and the Thanksgiving she was giving them. He'd never be able to thank her enough for making this day special for them. He barely scraped by for his siblings, and she was going above and beyond and making it look easy.

"Something smells yummy!" Trey yelled.

Tori stepped out of the kitchen wearing an apron that matched Meg's and a brown sweater that fit the holiday atmosphere. "Hey, you're here early." She stepped up to him and planted a kiss on the corner of his lips.

She laughed and wiped at his cheek. "Sorry. Merlot isn't your color."

Taylor laughed, and Megan slapped his shoulder with a scowl on her face. "Stop it, twerp."

Marcus gave a single, loud clap to get his siblings' attention. "Everyone gets a job. Report to Tori for orders."

Tori handed forks to Trey, knives to Taylor, and dishes to Meg. Marcus was last, and she waved him farther into the kitchen before asking, "Can you get the turkey out of the oven? It took both of us to get it in there."

Marcus accepted the potholders she offered and opened the oven door. "This bird is enough to feed an army, angel."

"I assumed we'd make two meals out of it. After lunch, we can play some games Meg and I picked up, and then eat again."

He hadn't thought of that, but now he could remember the few Thanksgivings he'd spent at his friends' houses growing up. Dakota's mom liked to make sandwiches with the leftover meat, and Brian's family had a tradition of eating salad on Thanksgiving night topped with turkey, ham, spiced pecans, and cranberry sauce. It'd sounded strange to him at first, but after a huge lunch, it'd been nice.

"Sounds perfect. Thank you for putting this together. They don't get a nice Thanksgiving like this from me. It's hard enough to get them to sit down at the table together."

Tori brushed his cheek and smiled. "I know. I wanted to do this, and it's been fun. I'm more of a food-on-the-go kind of person, so this was a challenge for me. Thank goodness Meg is a seasoned cook and walked me through the tough parts. We had a great morning."

Marcus pulled the turkey out of the oven and watched the kids talking around the table as if they hadn't fought all morning and wondered what could keep them happy like they were now. Thanksgiving was one day of the year, but he wanted this moment to last.

Tori stepped beside Marcus with a carving knife and a smile. "Get to chopping. It's almost ready."

Marcus led the blessing of the food before they ate until they were miserable and slumped in their chairs without making a decent dent in the food. Tori and Meg really went overboard, but the food was delicious. The boys wouldn't stop talking about it.

Meg chose Pictionary as the first game, and they found out that Marcus had a natural skill for drawing, but Tori couldn't draw a stick figure. Meg laughed until tears rolled down her cheeks when Trey drew what he claimed to be a raccoon.

Trey chose Charades next, and they all had a good laugh at Brandon, who thought he was too cool to act out his topics. Meg made sure to remind him he wasn't as cool as he thought he was, and there was a lot of eye rolling. Taylor found his calling as he put his best effort into every skit and carried his team to three wins.

When the sun went down, they made another full meal out of the amazing feast, and the kids sat around the living room draped over couches and recliners half asleep watching *The Nightmare Before Christmas*. The kids had cleared the table, but Marcus helped Tori clean up and watched his siblings across the large, open room that made up the kitchen, living room, and dining area. He'd never seen them so content together.

Tori tossed a dish rag on the island and said, "Looks like we're done" as she handed him a mug of steaming coffee.

He took it and pulled her closer to his side with a hand around her waist. "Look at them. I can't believe you did this. It's a miracle, Tori. This has been the best day."

Tori snuggled into his side, and he felt like everything in the world was right. "I've had the best day too. I never had this either growing up. I mean, my mom and I visited family, but we weren't really close to them. Having a full house has been amazing."

"You want to step outside for a minute?" He'd enjoyed hanging out with everyone today, but now, he wanted to be with Tori alone.

"Let me grab my coffee and a coat."

He opened the door and waited for her to exit first before following her into the cold night. The moon shown bright over the river, and the wind was light.

She stepped to the railing of the porch and leaned on her elbows to look out at the shining water.

When he stepped up close behind her without a word, she turned and looked up at him. "I really like it here." Her words were soft, but they were clear and sure in the quiet night. "This feels like a home, something I didn't know I was missing."

He stayed quiet as his mind celebrated her words. He wanted her to stay more than anything.

The thought alone of losing her was enough to choke him.

"Is this what it would be like if I stayed? There's not much waiting for me back in Chicago. I love my job, but I could be a nurse here."

Marcus couldn't breathe, couldn't move as he waited for her to finish.

"What if I stayed?" she whispered.

She'd asked, and he couldn't stay silent any longer. He took one step closer to her and slid his hands up both sides of her neck, barely skimming along her soft skin and up into her silky blonde hair.

He looked into those blue eyes that held the passion and fire he felt reflected in himself. His fingers tingled and his heart pounded in his chest. This was the biggest risk he'd ever taken. "What if I told you I'm in love with you? What if I said I want you to stay here, with me?"

Tori sucked in a breath and her mouth hung open in shock. He'd never asked for anything for himself in his life, but now, he had to hope, had to tell her.

"Because I do. I love you, and I want you to stay."

Tori covered her mouth with her hands, and her blue eyes turned hazy with tears. She slid her hands down her face and let them rest on his chest. He was sure she could feel his pounding heart through his coat.

"I love you too. I want to stay."

He leaned his forehead to touch hers and whispered, "Stay. Please stay."

She nodded her head against his and whispered, "I'm staying. I can't believe I'm staying."

Her shoulders shook with her sobs, but he leaned in and sealed her mouth in a kiss. She was the answer to his prayers, a chance to change the mediocre life he'd been living. He'd thank God every day for leading them to each other, and he deepened the kiss as his heart swelled. Never in his life could he have imagined a love like this was possible for him.

She wrapped her arms around his shoulders and pulled him closer. Her body was warm as she fit perfectly in his arms against the chilly night air, and he knew this would be the moment his life changed forever.

When they broke the kiss, he held her for long minutes as she laughed and cried. He brushed his hand over her soft hair and whispered, "Welcome home."

CHAPTER NINETEEN

Marcus

When the next weekend rolled around, Marcus was supposed to be in the lineup at Backyard Racing. He'd been worried about asking Tori to go with him, but she'd been the first one in the car. Who would've thought the city girl would be interested in dirt track racing?

Marcus and Brian had been a racing team for a couple of years, and the partnership worked well for both. Brian funded the car restoration, and Marcus raced and often won. They split the winnings and called it a good time.

Barbara or one of Marcus' friends usually kept an eye on the kids while he raced, but Tori stepped up and agreed to sit with them. Lindsey would be there too, so she'd have plenty of help, and Megan was spending the night with a friend, so there would be one less head to count.

Tori had stepped into his family and found her place in a hurry. It seemed the way to his siblings' heart was through their stomach because her Thanksgiving dinner had sealed her place in the hierarchy around the house. He'd noticed Meg asking Tori for permission to stay the night with her girlfriend earlier and wondered how he'd been demoted in his own family.

Marcus couldn't complain. He relished Tori's presence, and she was doing wonders for the family morale. He'd met with Trey's teacher earlier in the week, and she'd explained his brother's difficulties with his science lessons and sent home a remediation packet to be completed within the week.

Tori stepped up without being asked and spent hours with Trey every afternoon teaching him and taking the time to explain the biology concepts that flew over even Marcus' head.

Tori gave so much of her time to him and his family with ease, and he wanted to do something for her. He'd been thinking over a nice date in Atlanta, but his ideas all fell flat. Tori deserved the nicest dinners, long walks on the beach, and all that other romantic stuff women loved on TV movies.

Instead, he was taking her to a dusty racetrack to watch him crash a car into a dirt bank. The whole evening seemed beneath her, but he couldn't help noticing the smile on her face. They held hands as they walked into the arena, and the rumble of engines rattled his bones.

They herded the kids toward the metal bleachers and caught sight of Lindsey and Dakota sitting toward the top. Tori waved, and Lindsey stood to wave back. At least Tori would have a friend to sit with while he raced.

"Hey, I was worried you wouldn't make it." Lindsey grabbed Tori's hand as she sat in the empty seat next to her.

"Oh, you know, Marcus here sat around 'til the last minute worrying over asking me to come." Tori shoved her thumb over her shoulder at him. "He's afraid I'll bolt if I find out he's a good ol' country boy." She turned to look at him and winked as he took his seat beside her.

"My fears were valid. You've never been to a dirt track race before, and it might send you running back north."

Tori waved her hand in the air to dismiss his concerns. "This is fun. I'm having a blast. Plus, Lindsey and I have to talk about the Bible Study group I'm joining."

Marcus was shocked into stillness for a moment as Lindsey grabbed Tori's arm and started rambling about Tuesday nights and their curriculum. Lindsey had called him a few nights ago to let him know Tori had reached out to her about last Sunday's sermon and that she would be inviting Tori to join their women's Bible Study.

He'd been thrilled to hear Tori was asking questions, but he'd wondered if he should be concerned she hadn't come to him for answers. He'd started leading prayer before every meal and trying his best to make her feel comfortable in church. They often talked about the Sunday service and what they took from it, but he prayed for more. Seeing her accept Lindsey's invitation to the Bible Study settled something in his heart.

He let the women talk for a while, and soon Brian joined him to discuss race strategy. Marcus had trouble focusing on his friend's shop talk when Tori's arm kept brushing against his as she chatted with Lindsey.

About half an hour before Marcus was scheduled for a drivers' meeting, he turned to Tori. "You want a snack? The concession stand has nasty ballpark food, but I'll get you anything you want."

"I'll go with you. I want to see what they have."

Lindsey gave them a Cheshire cat smile as she gripped Taylor's shoulder. "I'll watch the little rascals. Bring me a Coke." Brandon had drifted off into the crowd with a friend, but Taylor and Trey still pestered each other to no end in the row in front of them.

"You got it," Marcus yelled as he grabbed Tori's hand to lead her down the bleacher stairs.

When they walked behind the bleachers toward the concession stand across the open dirt lot, Marcus asked, "Are you really having fun, angel?" He rubbed a circle on the top of her hand as they walked and realized his old instinct to keep quiet was born of a lack of companionship. He actually wanted to talk to Tori, and he'd never experienced anything like it before.

"Of course, this is the craziest thing I've ever seen. I can't believe this is really a thing."

"Oh, yeah. People love racing."

"I'm just wondering, why do you call me angel? At first, I thought it was a jab at me from the way you used it on the day we met, but you've somehow turned it into an endearment."

Marcus gave a half grin and asked, "Do you really wanna know?"

She rolled her eyes. "Of course. I asked."

"That first day we met, you were wearing all white, and that was the first thing that came to my mind when I saw you."

She chuckled. "You're such a romantic."

"No, really. I don't think I ever told you, but I'd had a tough day when we met. Seeing you standing on the side of the road in your perfect clothes and shiny blonde hair, you looked like an angel, or what I expect an angel to look like."

Their steps slowed as they approached the concession line, and she turned to him with a look of wonder.

He took her hands in his and turned them over, letting them lay open in his own as he said, "Look at you." His dirty, calloused hands engulfed hers. "Look around." She turned her gaze from their hands to take in the milling people waiting to be entertained.

When she turned back to him, his gaze locked on hers. "You don't belong here."

He watched her swallow hard as her smile fell.

"Women like you and men like me aren't meant to make it. My drug addicted mom spent her life in the foster system, and my dad left us without looking back." He whispered, "I come from a long line of sinners, Tori."

Marcus shook his head and continued. "Not you. You're better. You flew in from the City of Angels and landed here, of all places." He brushed her cheek with one hand and took a deep breath to ease the ache in his chest. "That day we met, you didn't seem like something from this world. You were straight out of my dreams, and I couldn't shake it—that feeling that you were different."

Tori's eyes were glassy, and she bit the side of her bottom lip as he asked, "Doesn't any of that scare you?"

Tori shook her head. "Not at all. You've shown me who you are." She looked up to the stands where his siblings waited for them. "You've got a track record that speaks for you. You've given your brothers and sister a home where they watch you work hard, treat them right, and live a Christian life. You don't scare me, you inspire me. You're a product of trial by fire, and you're not as insignificant as you make yourself out to be. I see you, and you look more like a phoenix than a pile of ashes."

He pulled her in close and whispered in her ear, "I love you. I wish we weren't standing in a crowd of people so I could kiss you." What she did to him, the changes she'd forged, were more than he could have expected.

"I love you too, but you can kiss me later. Right now, I need a hotdog." Tori playfully nipped at his ear as she grabbed his hand and pulled him forward in the concession line.

"I'll buy you as many hotdogs as you want, angel."

She gave him a closed-mouth grin and patted his cheek. "Always buy me food, and keep calling me angel. We'll have a long and happy life."

What he wouldn't give to have a lifetime of teasing and kissing with Tori. His entire life was sorting itself out with her in it.

They bought two hotdogs and two Cokes at the concession stand. Marcus could barely tear his gaze from Tori as they walked back to their seats. How had he gotten so lucky? He stepped to the side and waited for her to ascend the stairs ahead of him when Brandon's tall frame and white shirt caught his eye. His brother was sneaking into the tree line with someone, and Marcus knew he needed to keep an eye on him.

"Hey, take this to Lindsey, and I'll be right back. I need to check on Brandon."

Tori took the hotdog and Coke from him before kissing his cheek and turning back to the stairs.

Marcus couldn't control the chill that filled his veins as he stalked closer to the spot where his brother had disappeared into the cover of the trees. Every step he took away from Tori felt like a shove from the light into darkness. He knew in his bones that whatever Brandon was into wasn't good.

Marcus spotted Brandon just as the other man he was with reached to give him something.

"Don't touch it." Marcus' deep voice was strong enough to hold his authority, but low enough not to draw attention to their meeting in the woods.

The stranger cursed and ran in the opposite direction as fast as his legs could carry him just as Brandon backed against a tree looking like a deer caught in headlights.

Marcus stalked up to Brandon and patted him down. "What was it? Tell me. Now!" Marcus turned every pocket inside out and checked the waistband of his pants for good measure.

"Nothing. I… I didn't take anything." If Brandon's stuttering and wide eyes were a lie detector, his brother was guilty.

Marcus grabbed the collar of his brother's white shirt and pushed him back into the tree. "What in the world were you thinking? Drugs, Brandon? Did Mom put you up to this?"

"Um, she… I talked to her last week… and…"

"Spit it out."

"Nothing."

"Fine." Marcus released his brother's collar with another shove and grabbed him by the upper arm. "You're on lockdown until further notice. No phone, no friends, no TV, nothing." Brandon pulled against his hold, but Marcus dug his fingers into his brother's arm.

Marcus' temper was flaring, but he'd worked too hard to keep the kids from the life their mother lived. He wasn't about to let that demon sneak into the home he'd created for them.

Marcus dragged Brandon back to the stands kicking and screaming. Brandon was hitting his growth spurt, but Marcus was still taller and manual labor was his life. Once he wrangled his brother up the stairs, Marcus sat Brandon down in front of Dakota.

"This one," Marcus spoke to his friend and pointed to Brandon, "isn't allowed to move until I get back. He can wet his pants for all I care. Don't let him out of your sight."

The announcer called for the driver's meeting for the upcoming race to convene and Dakota gave a wicked smile as he slapped his hands down on Brandon's shoulders. "You got it, boss. We'll have a good time."

Dakota was built stout and strong, and Marcus knew Brandon would end up on the losing end should he choose to make a run for it. The hothead was crazy enough to make a go of it.

Marcus turned to Tori and grabbed her hand. "I'm sorry. I'll explain later, but we need to leave as soon as my race is over."

He kissed her hand, and she took the scene in stride. "That's fine. Good luck."

Would she be so calm about it when he told her what Brandon was likely getting into? Marcus walked to his car praying the whole way that God would show him the way to pull his brother out of whatever trouble he was getting himself into.

$\mathscr{C}$HAPTER $\mathscr{T}$WENTY

Tori

Tori spent her days remodeling and decorating the cabin while Marcus was at work. Sissy continued to be an asset, but Marcus' friends, Declan and Dakota, helped out with larger projects when they could. The two men owned a small contracting company, and Tori was happy to learn that Brian and Ian, a few of Marcus' other friends whom she'd met a few times, owned the hardware store in town.

Surrounded by helping hands, the cabin was taking on a life of its own. Now that she'd decided to stay, she was able to decorate the cabin the way she wanted it. Creating a true home with comforts was fun, but the house was often empty. She spent most afternoons at Marcus' house helping the kids with homework or dinner, and she knew the cabin was missing *life*.

She'd spent enough time in the hardware store to become familiar with the place, and Brian was always helpful when she couldn't find something she was looking for.

But Tori wasn't the only one building a home. Marcus' friends, and now her own friends, Jake and Natalie, were engaged to be married and building a house just outside of town. Tori and Natalie took turns helping each other out just for a change of pace.

Their mission for the day was choosing bathroom flooring for Natalie and Jake's new home. Tori and Natalie studied the samples while Jake and Marcus searched the hardware store for Brian to place the order.

"I prefer the slate color. The bathroom is large enough that it won't darken the room, and your shower tile has flecks of this color in it." Tori handed Natalie the shower tile sample Sissy had helped her choose the week before.

"I really like that one too. I think the master bath is really coming together. I'll take this sample and just ask Sissy later. We can order the shower tile now."

They wandered into the garden section, and Tori spotted a large, green plant with holes dotted in the leaves that were bigger than dinner plates. "Look at that! It's an indoor plant, and I have the perfect place for it."

Natalie leaned forward to read the information. "It looks cool. It would be perfect in that huge window you have in the living area."

Tori took the tag and decided to pay for it and ask Marcus to help her carry it out. They stepped up to the cash register, and Tori craned her neck to look for Marcus. "I wonder where the men got off to."

"Who knows? I know Jake could spend hours in this place," Natalie joked as she waved to the cashier. "Hey, David, you doin' okay?"

"Oh, yeah. I'm just fine. What about you?"

"Still building every chance we get." Natalie grew up in Carson, and it still amazed Tori that her friends knew everyone they met out in public.

David gave her a price for the plant, and Tori handed over her credit card.

"Hey, you're a Wright? There used to be lots of Wrights 'round here, but now I'm the only one left. Or at least I thought I was."

Tori felt a weight drop on her chest. A simple, "Oh," was all she could muster.

"Yeah, my crazy uncle cheated on my aunt with her best friend and the scandal was so big, my aunt and uncle packed up and moved to Chicago. Took my cousins with 'em."

Natalie laid her hand on Tori's arm and stepped closer to David. "Yeah, I remember that. Hey, do you think you can help us get that big plant to our truck?"

Tori said a prayer of thanks for Natalie's change of subject. The last thing she needed was to be tied to the Wright family when she was trying to make her new life here.

Before David could answer, a plump woman who looked to be in her early sixties stepped up beside Natalie with her hand on her hip. "I heard that Scott boy just had a scandal himself. You know, he's some big-time doctor up north, and his wife just cheated on him with another doctor! That Wright family is cursed, I tell you. Always havin' some kinda love drama."

Tori took a deep breath and said, "What?"

The old busybody went on. "Oh yeah, Scott was always a good boy. It's terrible he got caught up with some hussy from the city."

Tori sucked in a breath just as Natalie spoke up. "Ms. Miller, you've got to stop spreading rumors like that. You don't know Scott Wright from a hill'a beans."

The old woman, Ms. Miller, Tori thought, jerked back as if she'd been slapped and placed a hand on her heart. "Why, Natalie Burke. That's no way to talk to your elders."

"Don't pull that on me. I know good 'n well that Brother Jim has had to have a sit-down with you before about gossip. I know his phone number too, you know. Don't make me use it."

David handed Tori her credit card, but his attention was captivated by the exchange between Natalie and Ms. Miller.

Tori grabbed the card and tugged Natalie's arm. "Let's get out of here."

Tori turned around to make a quick exit and bumped into Marcus.

"Hey, what's goin' on here?"

Ms. Miller spoke up and pointed to Tori and Natalie. "Those two are disrespectin' me, and I don't appreciate it. Your mother would be ashamed, Natalie."

Jake took a step forward and Tori almost shrank from the look on his face. "Ms. Miller, you know better than that. I put up with a lot of your smart talkin', but I won't stand here and let you talk to Natalie like that."

"Well, I never—"

Marcus interrupted her innocent speech. "Yeah, we've heard it all before. Talkin' about someone's deceased parent is low, even for you."

Tori turned to Natalie and saw her face turn pink just as her eyes welled with tears that never spilled over, but Natalie held her shoulders high and walked away with Ms. Miller still chattering on about manners.

When they were out in the parking lot, Tori pulled Natalie into a bear hug. "I'm so sorry." Emotions poured through Tori that she'd never experienced before. Was this what it was like to truly care for someone else? Their pain became your own? Tori was quickly learning that having friends and being in a relationship was a series of ups and downs, but she was willing to weather the downs to experience the ups.

"I'm okay. That snake can't use my mom against me. I knew her better than anyone, and she wouldn't have let Ms. Miller talk to you that way either."

"Thank you for stepping in. It caught me completely off guard." She'd told Natalie a little about her divorce over the weeks they'd been renovating together, and they realized Natalie had been in Scott's younger brother's class in school.

"No problem. Hey, we forgot the plant." Natalie turned and handed the plant tag to Jake and Marcus. "Can you grab this plant for us? Tori paid for it, but it's pretty big and we couldn't carry it ourselves."

Marcus stepped up to Tori and put his calloused hands on her face. There were some things she loved about him that she couldn't explain. Those working hands were a testament to his drive, his motivation, and she treasured them more than he would ever know.

"I'm sorry about that. Ms. Miller can get pretty nasty, but she had no right sticking her nose in where it doesn't belong."

"I know. It's okay. I'm over it."

"And you deserve better than that cheating rat. I'd like to—"

Tori interrupted him and pushed him toward the store. "Go on before you say something you'll regret."

Tori and Natalie watched the men walk back inside and Tori sighed, her voice turning wistful. "Those two are the best." Natalie smiled.

The piercing wail of a child's scream overrode all other sounds in the parking lot, and they both turned to see where it was coming from. Fifty yards away, a young boy no older than ten or eleven stood over a man lying on his side.

Tori grabbed Natalie's arm. "Call for help."

Natalie pulled her phone from her pocket and dialed as she ran into the store. Tori turned and ran the opposite direction—toward the scream, the emergency, and the one who needed her help.

*C*HAPTER *T*WENTY - *O*NE

Marcus

"Marcus!" Natalie called his name.

Dread filled his middle when he saw her running toward them.

"Jake, a man collapsed in the parking lot, I think. Tori went to help."

Jake, who was a Cherokee County Deputy, rushed past Natalie toward the door, and Marcus ran to Ian's office. His friend, Ian, was a co-owner of the hardware store, but he'd been a Marine before he was a business owner. Between Tori, Jake, and Ian, whoever needed medical attention would have an arsenal to hold him over until an ambulance could arrive.

Marcus burst through the office door. "Ian, someone needs help in the parking lot. Tori and

Jake are out there now, but they might need another hand."

Ian pushed back from his computer and followed Marcus to the parking lot where they found Tori performing CPR on a man who looked to be in his late fifties. A young boy with short brown hair stood screaming beside an old blue truck with Natalie.

Giving Tori plenty of space to work, he made his way to Natalie. "Did you call 911?"

"Yeah. They're on their way. I can't get him to calm down." Natalie hugged the boy tighter and whispered shushes in his ear.

"Hey, buddy." Marcus squatted between the boy and the man on the ground. "This woman here is a nurse, and she knows what she's doing. It's her job to save people, and she's good at it."

The boy sucked in short breaths and continued to sob. Marcus asked, "Can you tell me what happened?"

The boy shook his head frantically.

"What's your name?"

"M-M-M-Mario." The boy sucked air between his teeth and let out another wail.

The boy could be Trey's age. "You go to Carson Elementary?" Marcus was reaching for anything he could to keep Mario from focusing on what Tori was doing to the man behind him.

"Yeah."

"You know Trey Channing?"

Mario finally took his eyes off the scene and looked at Marcus. "Yeah."

"He's my brother. Are you friends with him?"

The boy shrugged. "Sometimes."

"Yeah, Trey can be a little rascal sometimes. Can you do something for me? Could you maybe keep an eye out for him? Don't tell him, 'cause we don't want him to know he needs a babysitter." Marcus winked at the boy as if they shared a secret.

"Yeah." Mario nodded emphatically as if he'd been given a daunting task.

"You sure you can keep him on the straight and narrow? I mean, I wouldn't ask just anyone to help me. My brother means the world to me, and I think I can count on you."

The wail of sirens could be heard down the road, and Mario turned his attention back to the man. "Is he gonna be okay?" His voice was still shaky, but he could get his words out now.

"I hope so, buddy. My girlfriend is the best there is when it comes to helping people. Is he your grandpa?"

"My pop."

When the ambulance arrived, Tori passed the patient to the EMT and joined Marcus and Natalie with Mario.

"Is he gonna be okay?" The boy talked to Tori as if he knew her.

She crouched down to speak to him. "I don't know, but I did all I could. I think he had a heart attack, but I got to him quick. That's a good thing. Your scream helped me find him when he needed help."

Mario pushed past Marcus to wrap Tori in a hug, and his sobs renewed. Tori held the boy and stroked her hand over his hair. "These people are here to help too, but they'll take him to the hospital to make sure he has the best care."

Marcus had an idea and checked the cab of the truck for a cell phone. He found one sitting in the console, and it didn't have a lock screen. When he returned, the boy's cries had waned again, and Marcus asked, "What's your mom or dad's name? I'll see if I can get in touch with them."

"Tabitha."

Marcus found a recent call from Tabitha and pressed the button. It rang once before she answered. "Hello?"

"Hey, Tabitha, my name is Marcus, and I'm here with your son, Mario. His pop collapsed in the parking lot at the hardware store, and the ambulance is taking him to Southeastern Regional, I think."

Tabitha sucked in a breath and yelled, "What happened?"

"My girlfriend is a nurse, and she got to him first and performed CPR. She thinks it was a heart attack."

The woman burst into sobs. "Where did you say you are?"

"At the hardware store."

"I'll be there in five minutes."

Marcus put the phone back in the console and went back to Mario. "Hey, bud, your mom's on her way." The boy still clung to Tori as if she was his last hope, but he nodded at Marcus' words.

Marcus and Natalie sat with Mario until his mom arrived. Watching Tori comfort a young boy gave him an insight into her job he hadn't seen before. She threw herself into the situation and took control. She'd probably saved that man's life then turned right around and soothed a scared child. She'd kept a level head and did everything that needed to be done.

Tori wasn't the closed-off, disconnected person she portrayed. He could see she was capable of immense love and compassion. That connection she shared with Mario wasn't clinical. She was a nurturer, an innate caregiver, a mother by instinct. He, on the other hand, had been thrust into the father role years ago, and he still couldn't get it right.

Tabitha arrived red-faced and frantic. Marcus watched Tori calm her with a few words before she took her son and rushed for the hospital to check on her dad.

Once Tabitha's car was out of sight, Tori turned to Marcus. "I hope he makes it. I got her phone number, and she said she'd keep me posted."

He pulled Tori into his embrace. "Me too. You were great. I've never seen anyone so calm and determined in a situation like that."

"It's what I do." She whispered the words against his chest and didn't break their bond.

"You calmed everyone in a matter of minutes. It was... amazing. It's more than what you do, it's who you are. Don't ever tell me you can't connect with people. I just saw it, and I'm so proud of you."

She pulled away and looked up into his eyes. "I think I need to start looking for a job."

It was the last piece of the puzzle that would solidify her stay. He'd been waiting, wondering when she'd start applying, and now, he could breathe again. She was really staying, and he had every intention of making this a place she'd never want to leave.

CHAPTER TWENTY-TWO

Tori

Marcus kept his family close in the days after the emergency in the hardware store parking lot, and Tori couldn't blame him. Tomorrow was never promised, and she often saw the worst of it in her job.

While she was ready to get back into nursing, she was enjoying the ease of her life while she renovated the cabin. It was like a switch had been flipped and she was able to enjoy something she'd never thought to try before coming to Georgia. She'd hired a moving company this week to transport the rest of her things from Chicago that she'd been holding in storage. Her decision to keep the cabin was finally sinking in.

On Friday night, Marcus called her when he closed up shop and asked if she wanted to meet him for a "throwback date." She had no idea what that meant, but she was learning to roll with things as they came. Marcus would make sure they had a great time, no matter what kind of date they were on.

She pulled up at his house in her Mercedes around 6:00 that evening, and the December wind stung her face. Thankfully, she'd brought the flannel and fleece jacket that was becoming her lifeline in the unforgiving southern winter.

Stepping up to his front door, she thought about her old home in Chicago. It was nothing like the old, worn house before her, but Marcus' home had something her old loft hadn't touched. The place was inviting and always loud.

Tori opened the door and Meg came running down the hallway. "Tori!"

Marcus didn't have a quarter of the bank account she was accustomed to, but he had something more valuable she hadn't considered. Tori smiled as Meg wrapped her in a hug. Marcus' sister meant more to Tori than she ever expected, given her long-held indifference to children. After seeing the way Marcus lived, her heart was filled with thoughts of family and the happiness they shared.

It didn't matter what his home looked like. Marcus was living a life full of love that she'd been searching for her whole life. She didn't need *things* to be happy. The people around her filled her heart to the brim.

Just as Meg released her from the welcome hug, Marcus stepped around the corner, and she felt it—that settling inside her soul that meant she was home.

His short, dark hair was damp from his post-work shower, and he wore a blue T-shirt with a growling wildcat on the front.

Marcus wasn't a doctor, but she couldn't care less about how he supported his family. He made her happier than she'd ever known just by opening the door for her or carrying things for her without being asked.

He looked at her now as if she were more precious than gold, and sometimes, Tori caught the worry in his expression when she knew he was thinking of how he could lose her. In those moments, she knew she loved him with her whole heart, and she made sure to ease his concerns again and again.

Not only did he take care of his people, but he lived his life for Christ. He was doing a great job of leading his family to do the same, even if she caught Brandon huffing every time he had to sit with the family during the services since his strict grounding after Marcus caught him in a secretive rendezvous with a man at the race. The more she learned, the more she respected Marcus for being the spiritual foundation for his family, even when things were tough.

It would never matter to her where he lived because she knew now that she would live in a box if it meant going through life with the man walking toward her now. She was sure of his dedication and loyalty in good times and bad.

"Hey, angel." Marcus' smile sent a thrill through her middle as he wrapped her in his arms and kissed her dizzy.

"Eww!" Trey squealed as he ran off toward his room, and they both broke the kiss laughing.

"You ready for tonight?" Marcus rubbed his hands together as if he'd cooked up a tasty surprise.

"Um, I might be if I knew where we were going."

Meg jumped up and down on the balls of her feet. "It's the playoffs! Brandon is playing, and they're in the second round."

Marcus confirmed. "Yeah, Carson plays Indian Springs tonight."

"A football game?" Tori asked.

"Yeah. I said throwback. I meant like a high school date." Marcus' smile faded. "I'm sorry. I should have thought about it more, or at least asked you. I haven't even taken you out to a nice dinner yet. Fairs and races and football games aren't exactly romantic." He scratched the back of his head and turned his gaze to the door.

"Marcus, you know I'll have fun. Stop worrying about it. I've never been to a high school football game before. I'm excited."

Taylor let out a bellowing laugh just as Meg screamed, "What?"

Marcus tried to contain his laughter as he asked, "How did you get through high school without going to a football game?"

"I went to a private school. We didn't have sports teams, but we did have to participate in physical education classes."

Marcus and his siblings stared at her with unblinking eyes. Surely private school wasn't unheard of here in Carson.

Tori asked, "Why are you looking at me like that?"

"I just… I… Meg?" Marcus turned to his sister for help, but she shrugged her shoulders.

Taylor sat at the kitchen table and yelled, "Is that what you're wearing?"

Tori examined her jeans, tennis shoes, and flannel jacket before responding. "Well, yes."

Marcus pointed at his brother and his tone turned serious. "Stop being rude, Taylor. She looks great."

"I just mean she's wearing Indian Springs' colors. That ain't right." Taylor shook his head in mock disappointment.

Meg sucked in a breath and grabbed Tori's arm. "I have a sweater you can wear. It's really warm, but you could wear your jacket over it and people could still see the colors." Meg ran off toward her room and Marcus turned back to face Tori.

"Listen, you don't have to wear the sweater if you don't want to. You look fine in what you have on." He leaned in closer and whispered in her ear, "I'll take you to Atlanta next week, and we can have a nice dinner," sending chills down her spine that landed in her toes.

When she regained her composure from that tantalizing promise, she reminded him, "You don't need to take me to nice places. I'm really enjoying doing things like this with you and the kids."

Marcus raised one eyebrow and asked, "Sushi or Thai?"

Tori laughed. "I could eat either. I really don't care where we go." The volume of her voice dipped to a whisper. "I'm happy."

Meg returned with the sweater and showed Tori to the bathroom to change clothes. The sweater fit well, and her excitement hit a new peak as she stepped into the living room to model the new clothing.

Marcus' gaze was locked on hers once she finished her dramatic twirl.

"What do you think? Worthy of a night cheering on our boy?"

Marcus and Meg approved, and Tori knew Trey and Taylor wouldn't care enough to weigh in.

Marcus' booming voice echoed through the small house as he called for the kids to load up in the car. When they ran by him toward the door one by one, he stepped beside her and wrapped an arm around her waist. "That sweater looks good on you. The pearl earrings even look good with it."

She'd forgotten about her earrings when she changed. "Oh, I just—"

"Leave them. It's nice to know that city girl is still here too."

They walked to the car and she tucked her fists under her chin for warmth as he opened the passenger door for her. "I have a surprise for you and the kids after the game tonight. You think we could swing by my house later?"

He looked at her as if he could discern what kind of trick she had up her sleeve. "Sure. That sounds fun."

The ride to the game was filled with squeals and laughter from the back seat. One minute Taylor was irritating Meg, and the next Trey was bothering Taylor. Marcus threatened to turn the car around, but he couldn't keep a straight face as the back seat passengers shouted a chorus of promises of good behavior.

Tori wasn't anxious to jump back into the fishbowl of the Carson public eye after the incident with Ms. Miller and Scott's cousin, David, at the hardware store. She didn't want to know what the townspeople thought of her because she *cared* what they were saying. It mattered that she made a good impression here. Her love for this place where she was building a home grew every day, and while rumors wouldn't make her leave, they would make things uncomfortable for a while if they spread.

The excitement of the football game was more than she'd expected. The stadium lights lit up the night, and the cheers of the crowd almost drowned out the announcer's voice. They stood the entire game, and she was glad she'd worn her comfortable shoes. She was used to standing for long hours, but jumping and cheering on the concrete stadium bleachers was a whole new level.

Tori didn't understand the game at all, but Marcus pointed to the field and said, "Brandon is number twenty-three." She watched that royal-blue jersey and every move he made with anticipation. Waiting for the next great play the team made was half the fun, and she mostly fed off the excitement of the crowd.

Carson was only down by two points with two minutes left on the game clock, and the stadium was a churning ball of life as both sides yelled at the top of their lungs. Meg gave Tori a shaker at half-time, and they waved the blue and white streamers in the air. The rush was enough to keep her up through the rest of the night.

When Indian Springs made one last touchdown to win the game, Tori watched Marcus' cheering shift to concern as he sat down and covered his face.

She was still learning, and the highs and lows of opening up your heart to love in its entirety was exhausting. Marcus loved his brother unconditionally, and even she could imagine what a devastating loss like this could do to Brandon.

They already had the ugly uncertainty of the drugs their mother had exposed him to looming over their lives, and an emotional teenager was the perfect prey for that kind of danger.

Tori sat beside Marcus and wrapped her arms around his shoulders. The cheers around them died as a wave of muffled shouts rose from the other side of the stadium.

"He'll be okay. We'll make sure of it." She rubbed his back as he nodded. "Maybe the surprise I have for them tonight will take his mind off it."

Marcus turned to her with a look full of faith. "Thanks. I hope so. I can't help but worry about him. I can't let him end up like Mom." He rubbed his hands over his face. "Being the parent is tough."

"I know, but you're doing a great job."

Marcus texted Meg and told her to find Taylor and meet them at the exit. Trey wasn't allowed to go off with his friends yet, and he held onto Tori's hand as they pushed their way through the crowd toward the parking lot.

They waited on Brandon for about forty-five minutes, and Taylor ran off to grab any leftover hotdogs from the concession stand to hold them over. Tori had made a huge pot of chicken noodle soup earlier in the day, and she promised them as many bowls as they wanted after her surprise.

Meg went home with a friend, so they had room in the car for Brandon on the way home. Tori heard Marcus talking about after parties, but Brandon wasn't allowed to go, and the tension was humming when Brandon joined them in the parking lot.

They stopped by Marcus' house to let Tori pick up her car, and they followed her home. After the adrenaline spike from the game, she'd hit a dip only to be buoyed back up in anticipation of the look on their faces when they saw what she'd done.

She jumped out of the car when they arrived and ran inside before anyone else could get there and grabbed the remote that controlled the outdoor lights. Tori stepped back onto the porch and waited for everyone to get out of the car before turning on the Christmas lights. She'd spent all day hanging them, and every corner and edge was covered in twinkling red, green, and white lights.

Trey's scream filled the night air as he jumped and shouted, "Wow!" Taylor let out a deep "Whoa," and Marcus stood like a statue taking in the bright decorations.

She'd done it. She'd created the home she hadn't known she wanted, and the family to go with it was happy and excited. Her home was here, and tears welled in her eyes when she couldn't contain her happiness.

Marcus bounded up the stairs to her and wrapped her in his arms. "It looks amazing. I can't believe you did this."

She let his warmth seep into her body as her chin quivered. She was learning that it was possible to cry from happiness, and it was the most amazing feeling she'd ever experienced. "I love you," she whispered. It was the only thing that she knew right now.

"I love you too, angel."

God had led her to this wonderful place, and she closed her eyes to say a prayer of thanks. He'd been working in her life long before she knew to trust Him.

Trey and Taylor were comfortable enough in her home now to run past her and let themselves in. Tori didn't release Marcus as she heard both boys gasp when they found the decorations inside, and she squeezed Marcus a little tighter.

In that moment, her heart opened. She knew what was possible, and she knew how it had come to be. Without thinking twice, she knew she had to acknowledge the One who'd given her this gift.

"Marcus, will you pray with me? I mean, will you let me pray... out loud. This feels too important not to be confessed."

His hold around her became breathtakingly tight as he whispered, "Of course."

Tori drew in a shuddering breath and prayed, "My gracious Lord, I want to humble myself today. I want to open my heart to You." She paused to catch her breath. "I also want to thank You for what You've done in my life. I know now that I should trust You with my whole heart. Please forgive me. I should have given You my devotion sooner. Forgive me of my sins, Lord. I don't want to be that lost person anymore."

She stopped to gather her strength and words, and Marcus waited with her in the cold night air. "I'm unworthy, but I know love now—the true unfailing love You have for me. Please guide me to live in Your path and learn to serve You."

They stood in silence for a suspended moment before she whispered, "Amen."

Tori pulled away from Marcus' embrace and smiled through her tears.

Marcus cupped her face and let his forehead rest against hers. "I love you, Tori. I've never been in love before, but you're right. God has given me something special too, and I won't take you for granted. I'm glad He led you here. He must have known I needed you."

"He knew I needed you—all of you." She took his hand in hers and led him inside. "Come on, let's see the decorations and eat some soup."

Tori knew this night would be forever imprinted in her mind. The pull to her Heavenly Father was too great, and she was reborn. She couldn't wait to share the news with everyone she knew, and Sunday would be a great day when she could tell Brother Jim about her decision to accept Jesus as her Savior.

CHAPTER TWENTY-THREE

Tori

Tori spent the next day shopping with the girls. They'd planned the outing last week, and every one of her new friends were able to come. The objective was Christmas shopping, and Tori had to admit the task was daunting.

Since everyone knew everyone else, they all had ideas for gifts before the shopping trip began. Tori, on the other hand, spent too much time overthinking each purchase.

Some people were easier to buy for than others. Meg was easy, but it was hard keeping the purchase a secret from her while they were shopping together. Lindsey, Addie, Natalie, and Sissy were easy too, and she'd found Barbara a nice wall hanging.

Marcus' brothers were easy to buy for too. It didn't take much to understand the working of a preteen boy's mind. Brandon was a little tougher to figure out, but Meg assured her the gift she'd finally settled on would be perfect.

Lindsey let her know early on that the women only bought for their own boyfriends. They didn't want everyone breaking the bank on Christmas, and after a few years of gag gifts, the men just asked if they could play a friendly game of Christmas bingo instead of exchanging gifts. The men often played poker together on Wednesday nights without real money, so bingo played with small gag gifts was their way of mixing things up. They had an annual Christmas Eve party and there was a contest to see who could bring the craziest bingo gift.

Tori had something special in mind for Marcus, but she wouldn't find it in a mall. The project was taking longer than expected, but she and Meg had kept it a secret for a week now. Marcus thought they were planning outfits, but they'd really been working on a gift for him.

Once everyone had more bags and presents than they could continue carrying around the mall, Lindsey called it a day. "Okay, ladies, meet me at Rusty's in an hour."

Sissy saluted her friend with a sarcastic, "Yes, ma'am."

"Oh, and call the boys too. I want everyone there," Lindsey ordered as she led the tribe toward the parking lot.

A few of the women laughed, but no one objected until Sissy pulled her cell phone a few inches from her ear to say, "Tyler says he's gonna skip this one. I think I will too. I need to get home and see my girl."

Lindsey shook her head. "No, tell Tyler to meet us there and bring Lydia."

Tori adored Lindsey, and she found her pushy nature endearing. Tori assumed that was because she saw that same quality in herself quite often. Lindsey didn't take no for an answer when she wanted something. The girl was determined.

Sissy brought the phone back to her ear. "You heard the woman. We're going to Rusty's. Bring Lydia. I love you."

Natalie disconnected a call at the same time and said, "Jake is with Marcus and Declan. He said he'd let them know the plans."

That sounded like she could save her call to Marcus. She decided to text him instead.

You coming to Rusty's?

His reply was quick, and she smiled when she saw those dots on the screen that let her know he was replying.

I've been ordered to be there, but if you're going, I won't drag my feet.

I'll be there, and I'll bring Meg.

I love you.

She smiled and wondered how she'd become part of the perfect family in these last few months. Marcus and his siblings had accepted her into their life and their home, and she even had a circle of friends now—something she'd never experienced before. Her blessings were overwhelming, and she remembered the celebration she'd shared with the girls when she'd told them about accepting Christ into her heart last night.

She typed her reply with a prayer of thanks in her heart.

I love you too.

Marcus and some of their other friends were already settled in at a table at Rusty's when Tori and Meg arrived. She saw Marcus before he noticed them, and wondered how the dark, mysterious bad boy she'd met on the side of the road had turned into the smiling, bright-eyed man she saw now.

The moment when he turned and noticed her almost stopped her in her tracks. His moody gaze pierced her own and sent a jolt of awareness to her chest. This man was the love of her life, and every day was better with him beside her.

He stood to greet her and pulled out a chair beside him for her to sit. "Hey, angel. Did you have fun shopping?"

Meg took the lead and rattled on about the things they'd seen and the gifts they'd found, and Tori was grateful for Meg's growth. She'd found her self-esteem in the last few weeks, and it was a sight to behold.

The evening was filled with laughter and playful banter as their friends filled the table one by one. After an hour, half the restaurant was taken up by their friends, and Tori took a moment to look around and appreciate the gift she'd stumbled into. She couldn't have known that her divorce would lead her to happiness, but she'd accept the blessing with open arms.

Lindsey stood up and patted Dakota's arm beside her. He stood tall and proud next to his wife and wrapped his arm around her back.

Lindsey turned toward the sea of tables and friends and shouted, "Hey, everyone, we have something to share with you."

Dakota pulled something from his back pocket and handed it to Lindsey with a smirk. She took the photo from him and held it up for everyone to see. "We're having a baby!"

Tori saw the sonogram photo and reached for Marcus' hand just as Sissy jumped from her seat to hug her friend. Natalie squealed and Addie hugged her fiancé, Declan.

Tori didn't know how to react to her friend's happy news. It was too much, too soon, and her heart would burst in happiness. By the time she turned to Marcus, tears filled her eyes, but Marcus looked back to her with his brows drawn together in concern. Was he worried about *her* reaction to the news?

"I can't believe it." The words were almost inaudible, but Marcus must have heard her because he brought her hand he'd been gripping to his lips and kissed it.

She tried again, and this time, she was able to get the words past the lump in her throat. "They're having a baby. I'm so happy!"

She hugged Marcus, but quickly pulled away to seek out Lindsey and Dakota to offer her congratulations. Marcus was right behind her, holding her hand in the crowd that surrounded their friends.

They finally made their way to the happy couple and celebrated the news. A new little Calhoun baby would be joining them soon, and even baby Lydia was excited about the coming of her cousin.

Everyone eventually made their way back to their seats, and Brian and Addie took the stage for a while, singing upbeat songs to match the happiness that filled the restaurant.

About an hour into the celebration, Tori's phone buzzed in the back pocket of her jeans. Assuming it was her mother, she answered the call without looking at it.

"Hello."

"Victoria, it's Scott."

The shock at hearing her ex-husband's voice left her stunned, and she didn't reply. Whatever he wanted, he could get to the point or end the call.

"I'm in Atlanta for a lecture this weekend, and I'm coming by to grab a few things from the cabin. I failed to inform my mother that you were taking over ownership of the cabin, and she reminded me of a few things she'd left there she'd like to have back."

Tori didn't want to play nice, but she also didn't want to argue. It wouldn't do them any good, and while she wasn't thrilled to be having this conversation with him, she was moving past the hurt he'd caused her.

"When?"

"I'm on my way now. I'll be there in about half an hour."

"That's short notice, Scott. You can't just drop by without asking."

"Why not? It's my place."

Those words sent a fire into her blood that stole the end of each breath she tried to inhale. "No, Scott. It's not your house, and you'd do well to come to terms with that fact. I'm not at home right now."

"Can you be there in half an hour?"

His mind was made up, and he was pushing her into doing something just because she knew he'd already driven half the way to the cabin.

"I can be there in half an hour."

"I'll see you then."

Scott ended the call without a proper farewell, and she found that she didn't really care if he observed pleasantries with her. She wasn't the one who had any unkindness to make up for between them. If he chose to disrespect her, she wouldn't let it bother her.

When she turned back to the table, Marcus caught her attention with a hand on her arm. "Hey, you okay?"

"Yeah, I'm fine. That was Scott. He said he's in Atlanta for the weekend and wanted to stop by to grab a few of his mother's things from the cabin."

Marcus didn't show any sign of distaste at her news, and asked, "Did you tell him he could stop by?"

She knew Marcus trusted her to respect him and their relationship in any situation that involved another man. She'd never do anything to compromise what they were building together.

"Yeah, he manipulated the situation quite a bit. He was halfway here from Atlanta when he called me, so I need to get back to the house and let him grab his things. I've changed the locks since I moved in, so he doesn't have a key, thank goodness."

Marcus nodded and said, "Okay. I'll pay our bill and we can go."

"Oh no. You stay. I'll come back or call you when he leaves. You shouldn't have to leave because I do."

"But I want to go with you." Was that worry she detected in his voice?

"You know you don't have anything to worry about, right? You're the only man I want to be with, and I'd never jeopardize what we have. I just think I should do this on my own. Once he takes his mother's things, he won't ever have a reason to come back, and I need that closure."

He took her hands in his and raised one to his lips for a kiss. "I know. I just don't like him. He hurt you, and I can't let it go."

She lifted her hand to his cheek and stroked her fingers across the stubble that had grown there since his morning shave. "You *can* let it go. I think I have."

He planted a quick kiss on her lips and grinned. "Go. Do what you have to do, but call me as soon as he leaves."

"I will. I love you."

"I love you too." Tori said her good-byes to everyone and Marcus walked her to her car. She watched the headlights bathe him in a yellow glow as he waved good-bye, and she knew she was driving away from her future now so she could put her past to rest for good. As much as she hated the idea, she knew it had to be done.

She wanted a clean slate to build her future with Marcus upon, and after tonight, she would have it.

CHAPTER TWENTY-FOUR

Tori

Scott wasn't there yet when Tori got home, and she was thankful. She needed time to gather her wits for this meeting. Hopefully, he would know where his mother's things were and could get them quickly.

She didn't like that she'd had to leave Marcus and her friends for this, but she was determined to let this be the last time Scott drew her away from the man she loved. Scott was the last person she wanted to see, but she could do it just to be rid of him.

Busying herself was the best way to keep her mind off the meeting, and there were a few dirty dishes in the sink waiting for her attention.

She'd just finished drying the bowls when headlights shone through the bay window.

Tori met Scott at the door, but at least he had the decency to knock. After hearing the way he referred to the cabin on the phone earlier, she was afraid he would just walk in.

"Hey. Come in." She stepped to the side, and he walked past her. It had been months since she'd seen him, but he still looked the same. It was funny that she saw him differently after their divorce. Any respect she'd once had for him was gone since the night he came home and told her of his affair.

"You changed everything," Scott said.

She could hear his irritation, and she held her tongue as best she could.

"Yes, the place is mine now. I had every right to make changes."

Scott huffed a sigh. "I didn't come to fight. I came to get my things." He surveyed the room and the decorations with a scowl on his face. Garland hung on every shelving surface, lights twinkled around the windows, and a decorated tree took up one corner of the living room. "You decorated."

"Yeah, Christmas is coming up. That's what people do."

"The clutter won't help the place sell." Scott crossed his arms and pushed his chest out as he took in the Christmas scene, and his attitude did nothing to help her irritation.

"Can you just get the things you need?" She turned back to the laundry room that was just to the side of the kitchen. "I'll be in here if you need me."

Scott took the stairs, and she assumed the things he was looking for would be in the attic, the only place she hadn't cleaned and renovated.

He returned about fifteen minutes later with an old shoebox under his arm. "Why did you decorate? You never did anything like this at our loft."

"Because I'm staying, and I wanted to make this a home." Her civil tone was back after she had those fifteen minutes to calm down.

"You're kidding. There isn't anything for you here."

Tori felt the blow like a kick in the stomach, but she swallowed the ache. It wasn't true, but Scott didn't know that.

"There isn't anything in Chicago for me either. I already quit my job. I like it here, and I *do* have something here. I belong here more than anywhere else."

"This is crazy, Victoria."

"You don't have any control over my life anymore. It's not like you even cared while we were married. I love someone here. No, I love so many people here, and I'm finally happy."

"What?" Scott spat the word as if he couldn't believe it. To be fair, she'd never told him she loved him throughout their entire marriage. In those days, their relationship had made sense to her. Now, it sounded foolish.

"Yes. I've been seeing someone, so please don't call me again. You have everything you need now, and that should be the end of it."

"This is ridiculous, Victoria," Scott seethed as his gaze traveled down her body, then back up. "And what are you wearing?"

It took every ounce of her control to contain her sharp tongue. "What's wrong with what I'm wearing?"

Tori hadn't removed her flannel jacket when she'd arrived because she'd been chilled to the bone from just the walk from the car to the house. She tugged the jacket tighter around her and wished anyone else could understand what the simple piece of clothing meant to her. It was a sign that she could grow, that she could be comfortable being herself, that she'd found her home and it wasn't what she'd planned.

No, she saw now that God had bigger plans for her. She'd just needed to step aside and let Him work in her life, and the silly jacket meant she was learning to trust in things she didn't understand so she could become a better person, a better Christian.

Scott shook his head. "It's not you."

"This is me. It's not wrong to prefer comfortable clothes. I don't need the designer labels to be happy."

Scott scoffed and gestured to her outfit. "I don't even know you."

He was right. He didn't know her. In fact, until she came here, she didn't even know herself. Coming here brought her happiness and love, but it also brought her a realization of self.

Not only did Scott not know the person she really was, she knew she could say the same about him. She hadn't even known about his family and this cabin until after their relationship had died. She knew more about Marcus than she'd ever known about Scott in all their years together, and it was because she was able to see what love truly meant with God in her life.

"That's okay. You don't have to know me." Tori turned toward the wall of windows in the living room when she saw headlights bobbing up and down and smiled.

Being around Scott had her stomach twisted in knots, and she knew she'd feel better with Marcus beside her. She was glad Marcus hadn't listened to her and let her handle this all on her own. They were a team now, after all, and she was stronger with him beside her.

"Are you expecting someone?" It was barely past 8:30, but Scott's tone suggested a much later rendezvous.

No, she hadn't been expecting someone. How could she have been expecting someone like Marcus to come into her life and shake up everything she thought she knew about herself and the life she was living?

She hadn't been expecting Marcus to barge into her life the way he had, but she was glad he did.

Tori tried to hide her smile as she said, "Yeah, my boyfriend."

CHAPTER TWENTY-FIVE

Marcus

Waiting for Tori to call was a type of madness Marcus hadn't experienced before. Sure, he worried about his siblings every moment they were out of his sight, but somehow Tori had become one of those few people his thoughts revolved around.

He wasn't sure how she'd snuck her way into his heart and planted her roots so quickly, but he knew he loved her like his own family when that familiar panic crossed his mind every time he wondered if she was okay.

Marcus stabbed his straw up and down through the ice cubes in his glass of water as he waited. The only things he'd ever cared about for sure in his life were Christ, family, and cars. Now,

Tori just felt like part of the family category, and not knowing what was happening while she met Scott at her house was eating away at Marcus' patience.

He'd known Scott from school, even though Marcus was a few years younger. Scott's family had been prominent in the community. His dad was a family doctor and his mom was a nurse in his office, and they'd been known for their philanthropy around Carson.

When Doctor Wright cheated on his wife, the scandal had been too much for her to bear. The rumors suggested she'd forgiven him and decided to give their marriage another shot… if he agreed to leave town. So they'd loaded up the family and moved somewhere up north.

Marcus hadn't asked about the current condition of Scott's family, and he honestly didn't care. Marcus was firmly against judging someone by their parents' actions, but something had been nagging at him since Tori told him what happened to her marriage. Why did Scott cheat on Tori after seeing what his father's infidelity had done to his family?

Marcus liked it when he could understand people and the decisions they made, but he couldn't fathom why Scott had cheated on Tori. He got the sense that their relationship was strained and distant, but, to him, that wasn't a reason to break your marriage vows.

He checked his phone again to make sure it hadn't died or lost service. Nope, thirty minutes without word. Maybe that wasn't enough time. He could wait a few more minutes… he thought.

Addie rested her guitar against the stage wall and descended the short stairs as Brian began singing "Ask Me How I Know" by Garth Brooks. Marcus tried to focus on the song, but that was only making his wait worse. The words poked at him, prodding until he couldn't sit still.

Marcus tapped the heel of his boot against the floor, trying to release some of the building pressure that felt as if it would lift him from his chair. What was he doing here? Tori was alone, and after seeing the way she'd cried about Scott's betrayal that night he brought her home from the bar, he knew she could use the support he could give her. He didn't want her to face that pain alone.

When he couldn't contain himself any longer, he stood and made his way to Lindsey. Brian hadn't even reached the first chorus yet, but he knew it was time to go. He offered his congratulations then found Barbara.

"Hey, would you mind taking the kids home on your way? I'll be there soon myself, but I have somewhere to be first."

Barbara gave him a knowing smirk and patted his arm. "I don't mind at all. I'll even stick around until you get back. I don't have any other plans tonight. I'll make sure Trey gets in bed. Just do what you need to."

"Thanks. I'll call you later."

She waved as he turned to push his way through the crowd. He'd made the decision to leave at the right time. He knew he couldn't stand being here another minute.

The headlights cast their beams along the straight road leading to the cabin, and his mind drifted to Tori. If he couldn't be there with her now, he could still pray that she was handling everything okay.

Marcus let the plea resonate in his heart as he drove. In the quiet years of his life, he'd prayed often like this—silent and without a fuss. He found comfort in knowing he could take his troubles to God without announcing them to the world. His hopes, worries, and thanks were for the Lord's ears, and he shared them often.

He prayed she'd have the peace to handle seeing her ex-husband tonight. He asked God to give her strength and patience. He prayed the pain that Scott's betrayal had left in her heart would die, leaving room for the growth they were sharing with each other.

A car he didn't recognize sat in the driveway beside Tori's Mercedes when he arrived, and he parked behind Tori's car. Hopefully, Scott's rental car would be making its way back to Atlanta very soon.

Marcus bounded up the porch stairs and stopped short when Scott opened the door. Marcus couldn't speak as he took in the changes to the boy he'd once known. Scott's hair was thinner, and he could even make out gray patches above his ears in the light shining from inside the house that cast a shadow over his face.

So, this was the man who'd hurt Tori? The one who hadn't appreciated and loved her the way she deserved?

Tori appeared behind Scott, and Marcus knew that stern look on her face. She wasn't happy, and any patience she'd had was long gone. "Scott, you can't answer the door here. This isn't your place anymore."

Marcus couldn't help himself. Seeing Tori upset twisted the ache and worry in his chest into that warmth that he'd come to know as unfailing, unfaltering love.

He looked past Scott to Tori and winked. "Hey, angel."

"What are you even doing here?" Scott sounded like a disgruntled father, and Marcus almost couldn't contain his laugh at the question.

"I came for my lady." Marcus moved forward and reached for Tori's hand as Scott stepped aside.

Scott's gaze darted between the two of them as he asked, "At this hour? What could you possibly be doing?"

"Well, we were celebrating before you interjected yourself into Tori's plans for the evening," Marcus answered.

Scott turned to her and threw his arms in the air. "Seriously, Victoria?"

"Victoria?" Marcus asked. "So formal."

Tori's lips formed a thin line as she tried to contain her laughter. At least that tension he'd seen in her eyes when he'd arrived was gone.

"Of all the people, Victoria. What could you possibly see in Marcus?"

Tori held up her hand to halt his rant. "I didn't get a say in who you cheated on me with, left me for, or married. So, it's only fair that you leave my dating decisions up to me. What I'm doing here in Carson or with Marcus is none of your business, and I believe you were just leaving before Marcus arrived." She gestured to the open door and pulled her jacket closer around her body as the cold December air rushed in.

"Victoria!"

The minute Scott raised his voice, nice Marcus left the building. "I suggest you be on your way." The authority in Marcus' voice was heavy, and Scott's posture drooped the slightest bit.

"I'll do what I please, and I don't need you telling me what to do." Scott clutched the box under one arm and propped his other hand on the open door.

Marcus took one step closer to Scott and whispered. "You can't come into her house barking orders and insulting her. You have one more chance to leave peacefully. I suggest you take it, and heed her words. Don't come back."

Scott's gray eyes stared back at him as one second, then two passed before he nudged his way past Marcus and out the door.

"Have a nice life, Tori. You won't be hearing from me again." Scott didn't turn back as he got in his rental car and drove away… out of their lives for good.

CHAPTER TWENTY - SIX

Marcus

Marcus had Tori wrapped in his arms before Scott was out of the driveway. "Are you okay?"

She nodded her head against his chest and whispered, "Yeah."

Marcus knew Tori was independent and strong, and he prayed she would understand that the reason he'd come running had nothing to do with weakness… unless it was his.

"I'm sorry I didn't let you do this by yourself like I said I would. I wasn't doing a good job of sitting around waiting for him to leave." Marcus released a slow, deep breath. "It was killing me to stay away."

Tori leaned back to look at him. "I'm glad you came. I needed some support, and I wasn't

handling things very well before you showed up.
You calmed me."

Marcus looked into her blue eyes and
knew that he'd found something with her that the
world outside of the two of them couldn't touch.
He never thought he'd be able to trust someone
enough to have a relationship. Letting someone
into his life meant letting them get close to his
family too, and protecting them had always been
more important than any desire he'd had for a
date.

Now, he knew he didn't have to
compromise his family's safety with Tori. She
was good for him, but she was even better for his
family. Meg loved her, and the boys listened to
her because she always had their best interests at
heart.

Looking at her now, he knew he'd been
waiting for her. Tori was the most beautiful
woman he'd ever seen, and she understood him.
She knew his motivations, his drive, and his
priorities. She respected him and his
responsibilities enough to solidify their
relationship.

"You want some coffee?" she asked as she
stepped toward the kitchen.

He took in the elaborate decorations that
covered every square foot of the house. "I'll take

a cup. I still can't believe you did all this. These decorations are amazing."

She handed him a steaming mug and smiled as she lifted her own to her lips. "I know. I haven't ever decorated for Christmas before, so I just bought everything and put it… everywhere."

"Did you hear the kids when they saw it? They haven't ever seen something like this up close. Only in movies."

She took his hand and led him to the couch. The Christmas lights cast a holiday glow about the entire room and illuminated her smile. "I know. I haven't either. That's why I wanted to do this… for all of us. I didn't want them to be in their late-twenties like I am and wondering why Christmas didn't seem like the celebration everyone else made it out to be when I could give them something to help build the excitement. Plus, Christmas means more to me this year. It's more than lights and presents. We're celebrating Christ's birth."

Tori was right. The presents hadn't ever meant much to him, but the real meaning of the celebration was something he was thankful for every day.

Marcus sat beside her on the couch and pulled her close. "You have a kind heart, you know that?"

She chuckled. "I don't know. Scott seemed to think I'm not worth much tonight. I guess that's my fault. I wasn't my best self when we were married."

"I don't care if you were a mediocre version of Tori Sanders, you don't deserve to be talked to like that *or* cheated on. Ever."

"Thanks. That means a lot, but you don't know how I was before coming here."

He rubbed his hand up and down her arm. "Oh, I think I have an idea. I met this woman on the side of the road one time, and she was a total pain in the neck."

Tori swatted his chest and conceded. "Yeah, I heard about that. She wasn't so bad, was she?"

"Nah." Looking at her took his breath away. He was drawn to her in ways he couldn't explain as he leaned in and stopped a mere inch from sealing his lips against hers. "I love her."

Tori erased the space between them and wrapped her arms around his neck as she kissed him. Warmth flooded his chest and pulsed through his body with every beat of his heart. He didn't understand how she elicited the responses from him that she did, but no one else had ever made him feel so important and worthy.

Tori pulled away smiling. "I love you too." She dragged her fingernails along the stubble on his jaw and asked, "What did you think about Dakota and Lindsey's announcement tonight?"

"I'm happy for them. They were so close when we were young and all through high school. It almost broke Dakota when she left."

Marcus hadn't understood the pain Dakota went through when Lindsey moved to New York after high school, but now, he had a small sense of what losing the one you loved could do to a person.

"He was just starting to get his life back in order when she came back to town when Lydia was born. It's a good thing they realized what they had. They're much better together."

Marcus hadn't been able to understand why Dakota couldn't move on after Lindsey left, and he felt guilty for being hard on his friend in the years after she'd moved away.

"I think so too. They seem so happy together, and now they're having a baby."

He heard the wistful lilt in her voice and the question he'd been turning over in his mind all night gnawed at his insides. "What do you think about kids?"

"What do you mean?"

Marcus rubbed the back of his neck and asked, "I mean, do you… want to have kids someday?"

She hesitated and he realized he had no idea which way she would lean. It wasn't a make or break answer for him either way. He would respect her decision, whatever it may be, but he knew which side of the line he would lean.

He also wondered if his ready-made family would one day scare her away. Their relationship would never be "normal" because the life they would build together would include four other people and their futures as well.

"I think… I think I would like to have kids." She picked at her fingernails and nodded. "I never thought I wanted kids, but I love your brothers and sister. They're so wonderful."

Marcus kissed her forehead and knew he would do everything in his power to give her the family she wanted. Sure, he was tired of spending his days worrying about the kids he already cared for, but he knew Tori would make a great mom.

"But… I really like our family the way it is. Is it okay if I think of myself as part of your family?"

"You *are* part of my family, and I think our family is perfect the way it is too." He wasn't sure how she'd read his thoughts, but, once again, he was thankful they could be honest with each other.

"I mean, it'll be another eight years at least before Trey goes off to college. You've been a parent for most of your life, and I wouldn't blame you for wanting to enjoy some empty nester years. What about you? Do you want more kids?"

"I don't know, but I would have kids with you if that's what you wanted. You'd make a great mother."

She patted his leg and smirked. "You know, we don't have to figure this out tonight. We can talk about it again when Trey's a little older. If we decided not to have more kids right away, maybe we could foster."

"Are you making plans for years down the road?" An endless future with Tori was the extent of his dreams, but they'd always seemed like *his* dreams. Hearing her talk about things he'd only thought about alone felt amazing.

"Yes. Wasn't that what we were just doing?"

He brushed his fingers through her soft blonde hair. "I wish I could give you a traditional family like everyone else. I'm sorry about my baggage."

Tori pointed a manicured finger at his face. "Never apologize for your family."

Marcus let his hand fall from her hair. "You're right. I'm sorry."

"Listen, I love you and your ready-made family. You're giving me more than I ever imagined just by loving me. Now, I don't want to hear any more talk about your family or your job or your income like they're bad things."

She put one hand on each side of his face and looked into his eyes. "I don't care that you're a mechanic or a guardian to your siblings. You're realer than anything I've ever known, and how you make your money or the responsibilities you have at home doesn't change what you mean to me. I would choose you over every billionaire in the world because you're my person—the one I love doing life with."

She wound her arms around his neck and pulled him close. He was blessed beyond measure, and he didn't have a way with words, so she would never know how much she meant to him. She'd given him more of what matters in life, more times like this with his arms wrapped around her. That's what he wanted. He wanted to keep looking into her eyes every day and see that drive that told him she would always be by his side.

Tori whispered against his neck, "You came for me. You came for me when I was afraid of the storm, and you came for me tonight. You always know when I need you."

Maybe he could give her what she needed. He was a protector and provider, and that meant more than where he went to college or who his parents were. He meant something to this woman, and she was what he'd been missing—someone to share his life with.

He pulled her in close and promised, "I'll always come for you when you're scared."

*C*HAPTER *T*WENTY - *S*EVEN

Tori

Tori checked her ivory sweater in the mirror and continued applying her makeup. It had been days since she'd worn mascara, and it was nice knowing she didn't need to wear it unless she wanted to.

Tonight was special, and she wanted to go the extra step since Marcus was doing the same for her. He'd been insisting on a dinner date in Atlanta, but Marcus hadn't felt comfortable leaving town since Brandon was grounded after sneaking off to meet someone in the woods at the race a few weeks ago.

Marcus had allowed Brandon to have his phone for his birthday this past week, but he was still grounded. After waffling back and forth for days about their date, Marcus finally decided he'd never know if he could trust Brandon until he gave him a chance.

Satisfied with her makeup, Tori grabbed her black pea coat from the closet. They were well into the harshest winter Georgia had seen in a decade, and tonight was the first time she'd taken the designer coat off the rack. As cute as it was, it just didn't fit with the new clothes she'd been wearing, and she was okay with that fact.

Her phone rang just as she slid her arm into the sleeve of the coat, and she answered when she saw it was her mother.

"Hey, Mom."

"Hey, I hope I didn't catch you at a bad time."

"Not at all. I'm just waiting on Marcus to pick me up for our date tonight."

"What will it be this time?"

Tori had shared every crazy adventure Marcus had taken her on with her mother, and they marveled at the fun Tori had for days after.

"You might be disappointed in this one. It's nothing as exciting as the fair or a race. We're just having dinner in Atlanta."

"Well, that will be nice for both of you. I know you've been busy renovating the house and

Marcus works long hours. It's nice to take some downtime."

"I know, and I know I'll have fun with him wherever we go. I tried to tell him I don't need to drive an hour for exotic food. I can make Thai food at home. Well, I can *try* to make Thai food. I'm still learning how to cook anything, so I might be reaching with that one."

Her mom clicked her tongue on the other end of the line. "Oh, don't give me that. You told me all your meals have gone over well so far. You can't win them all, but you've had a great first run from what you've told me."

"No one has complained so far, but Meg has been a lifesaver more than once. She really knows her way around a kitchen, and Natalie shared a few of her easier recipes with me too. Everyone says she's the best cook around."

"Sounds like you're doing great."

"I am. Oh, and I forgot to tell you, I booked your flight today. I e-mailed the itinerary to you. Did you get it?"

"I haven't checked my e-mail today, but I'll let you know if I didn't. When am I flying in?"

"The twenty-third. You'll have half a day to get settled, and we'll spend Christmas Eve with my new friends… or the ones who can make it.

Some of them have family obligations, but most of us are going to Dakota and Lindsey's house for a Christmas party."

"Are they the ones having the baby?"

"Yes! You're going to love them. And you'll get to meet all of Marcus' siblings."

"I can't wait. You've told me so much about them, I feel like I already know everyone."

Tori halted her pacing and sat down hard on top of the quilt she'd purchased for her bed last week. "I can't wait for you to meet Marcus." Tori wrapped a curled strand of her hair around her finger and said, "I love him so much. I think he's the one. I never thought that about Scott, and I know why."

"I get it, honey."

"Marcus is the one I was always supposed to be with. I can't believe we found each other, but I know my life was always meant to have him in it."

"It sounds to me like your relationship with Marcus is completely different than what you had in your last marriage."

Tori squinted against the reminder of her failed marriage. It had been wrong from the beginning, and she'd been too selfish to see it. And yet without it, she never would have met Marcus.

"I'm happy you found Marcus. I'll always love you, and it's hard being so far away from you. I like knowing you're happy and loved by someone close by."

"Trust me, Mom. I have more love here than I know what to do with."

"I know you've always been hesitant to let people in, but I'm glad you're opening up. I thought your divorce would set you back even further, but I'm thankful I was wrong. It's not fair to judge a new relationship by an old one, and I'm proud of you for figuring that out on your own. If your heart recognizes its companion in someone else, you shouldn't ignore it because you're afraid of what might happen."

Tori wondered how much of her mother's words were meant for her and how much her mom was trying to convince herself to move on. It had been decades since Tori's dad left them, but her mom hadn't remarried or really dated anyone.

"You know I want that for you too, Mom."

Her mom huffed a sigh. "I know, baby. Maybe I should pack up and move to Georgia. I hear it's a pleasant way to meet the man of your dreams."

Her mother's chuckle was pleasant, but Tori was stuck on her words.

"That's a great idea. You should just come live here."

"Oh, don't be silly."

"Why? Because you have so much waiting on you in Chicago like I did?"

"I have a job, Tori."

"You're a chemistry professor. They have schools here."

"Not universities."

"The cost of living is much lower. Just look into it. It would be amazing having you here, and I think you'd love it. You could come to church with us, and you could join our Bible study."

"I'm so proud of you, Tori. Just hearing your excitement makes me think I could move on a dime. You know, I plan to retire in a few years. Maybe I can spend my golden years in a cabin on Wetumpka River close to you. I could take up painting again."

"And who knows, if things work out with Marcus, you'll have more family here."

It was all coming too fast. Her relationship with Marcus was an unexpected blessing, she had more friends than she could have imagined, and she'd just accepted a job at a local family practice in town and couldn't wait to tell Marcus tonight. Now, imagining her mother here by her side to experience it all with her was more than she could comprehend.

"You don't know what kind of blessing that would be." Her mom's voice grew unsteady as she continued. "It's always been just the two of us. Having more family to love would be wonderful."

Tori hadn't thought about her mother's feelings when she'd spent all those years putting off even the thought of having kids.

"Carson seems like the place where you've found yourself. It must be something special to be called your home now."

Maybe her life needed to fall apart to be put back together. If she'd known sooner, she wouldn't have fought against the huge change that was happening in her life that led her here.

"I have to go, but I'll call you tomorrow and let you know how the date went."

"I love you, Tori. See you soon."

"Love you too."

Tori heard Marcus' Mustang winding up the driveway just as she stepped off the last stair into the living room. Every time she walked downstairs, the Christmas decorations stole her breath. She'd missed out on so much happiness in those years she'd spent with her head in a book through school and working long hours just so she could crash in a drab loft in a city of anonymity.

Tori didn't try to beat him to the door. She knew Marcus liked knocking and escorting her to the car. His sense of responsibility for his family had kept him from delving too far into the dating scene, and he'd told her he enjoyed the slight formalities of picking her up for dates.

She let him knock before opening the door, and his smile matched her own as he said, "You're so beautiful."

"That's some greeting you've got there." She kissed his lips but didn't linger as she stepped around him and closed the door behind her. "Where are we going?"

"I talked to Brian's mom, and she gave me a few options. She works in Atlanta and knows all the good places."

"I'm really up for anything, and we don't need to make such a big deal out of a date. I love you, with or without the Thai."

"So, Thai? I know just the place." He winked at her and pulled her close to whisper in her ear as they descended the porch steps, "And I love you too, angel."

CHAPTER TWENTY - EIGHT

Marcus

Marcus opened the passenger door of the Mustang for Tori when they arrived at the restaurant. The place wasn't fine dining, but he'd asked Donna, Brian's mom, to leave the white tablecloth locations off the list for a reason. It wasn't that he didn't want to give Tori the best experience; it was that he wanted them both to have fun. Relaxing and fine dining didn't always go hand in hand.

He extended a hand to her, and she took it as she settled one sleek boot on the asphalt outside the car. Gently tugging, he guided her up and closer to him as she stood. Even in her heeled boots, he was still a few inches taller than her, and she tilted her head up to look at him.

"Are we going inside, or are you going to be staring at me all night?"

Her playful jab had him wrapping an arm around her waist to pull her in closer. "Didn't anyone ever tell you patience is a virtue?"

Tori tapped her slim finger against her cheek as she pretended to ponder his question. "You know, it sounds familiar."

Marcus gave a single huffed laugh and kissed her neck right below her ear. "Let's go get you some of that exotic food you like."

Tori rolled her eyes. "Thai food isn't that exotic. It's readily available in almost every city in America."

Marcus held the door open for her and shrugged. "Whatever you say, angel."

The dinner was everything he'd hoped it would be. Tori smiled, told stories about her mom and growing up in Chicago, and gave him updates on the changes she'd been making to the house. He could see her anticipation mounting as she spoke.

By the time the bill was paid, they were stuffed and happy as they walked back to the car. "You know," Marcus began, "I never really dated much. Most girls in high school didn't give me the time of day, and after that... well, I could tell women were just curious."

"About you?" Tori asked in mock surprise. "I can't imagine why. I mean, your brooding bad boy persona is like an open book."

He squeezed her hand and shook his head. "You get it. They were impressed until they figured out they weren't the center of my attention. By that time, I already had guardianship of the kids, and there was no turning back."

Tori rubbed his arm and leaned her head against his shoulder. "They don't know what they're missing."

He kissed the top of her head. "I'm not sure anyone knows that except you."

"Let's keep it that way."

"Yes, ma'am." He opened the car door for her and made his way to the driver's side.

The ride home was quieter. They were drowsy and dark had completely fallen. Marcus watched the headlights guide them home and his mind wandered to the kids. He didn't like leaving them home alone at night, but Meg assured him she'd call at the first sign of trouble.

Tori patted his leg. "You thinking about the kids?"

"Of course."

"They're responsible, Marcus. You taught them that."

"I know, and I know they need the responsibility, but I'll always worry. Brandon is grounded for a reason, and I can't understand why he would do something so stupid. I've tried so hard to give him the best I can, and it wasn't enough to protect him."

"You did great. Brandon hasn't caused a bit of trouble since. I think it's sinking in for him. Maybe some responsibility will be good for him."

Marcus' phone rang in the console between them, and his breath stopped. "Will you put it on speaker?"

Tori pressed the button and held the phone between them. "Hey."

It was Meg, and she didn't miss a beat after his greeting. "Marcus, Loraine just showed up. She's… I-I-I don't even know. She was crying and wailing about missing Brandon's birthday, and we couldn't calm her down. Brandon took her in his room, and I can hear her crying."

"We're about thirty minutes away. Can you call Jake? Just tell him to come over. He'll know what to do."

"Okay."

"Call me right back."

Tori disconnected the call and neither of them said anything at first. He'd had a feeling something would go wrong tonight. Their date had been too perfect. He pushed the accelerator toward the floorboard as his tension grew.

"Slow down. Getting us killed won't help them any faster."

"Sorry. Loraine never stops by, and she's never cared about missing a birthday before. I'm sure she realized it when she was sober and got high when she felt bad about it. I don't want Brandon or any of them having to deal with her. I try to keep it away from them."

Tori nodded and stared out the windshield.

Almost eight minutes had passed by the clock on the dash when Meg called back, and she was even more frantic than the last call.

"Marcus, I'm scared. Now Brandon is yelling too, and he locked his bedroom door. I called Jake, but he's fifteen minutes away."

Marcus punched his fist against the steering wheel. "I'm coming, Meg. I'll be there as soon as I can. Go ahead and call Dakota and tell him to come help."

"Okay."

His sister sounded unsure, and Tori leaned closer to the phone she held between them. "Meg, you can do this. We're coming. Just stay with your brothers until we get there."

"Okay."

"We love you." Tori said the words like they were second nature, and any calm Marcus had been holding onto burst like a water balloon in his chest.

"I love you too," Meg whispered before ending the call.

When they finally pulled into the drive, Dakota was just turning in behind them, and they all rushed to the door. Marcus could hear Brandon screaming, "Mom!" before he reached the porch, and he knew whatever Loraine had done was worse than he'd imagined. Brandon hadn't called her Mom since he was eight years old, and the sound his brother was wailing into the dark house was full of pain and almost incoherent.

Marcus burst through the door and saw Meg sitting between Trey and Tyler on the couch. She had one arm around each of them, and their faces were tucked into her shoulders. His sister shook with sobs as tears rolled down her wet cheeks.

"I don't know what happened!" Meg screamed to be heard over Brandon's wail.

Marcus was at Brandon's door in a few long strides with Tori on his heels. Marcus beat his fist against the door and he yelled, "Brandon, Brandon, open the door. It's me."

He heard Brandon scrambling for the door a mere second before it sprang wide open. His brother's soft brown hair was tousled, and his face was wet and red. Veins protruded from his neck as he screamed, "I think she's dead!"

Tori pushed past him into the room just as Marcus pulled Brandon out of the doorway into the hall. His tall, teenage brother cried gut-wrenching sobs into Marcus' shoulder as he reached to close the door where Tori had just kneeled beside their mother.

Of all the hurt their mother had caused them, of all the terrible things she'd done to them, this would forever be the pinnacle of the wrongs done to her children. Loraine was the worst mother, but as Brandon's arms held tight around Marcus' torso, he knew she'd just made her final stand.

All the years he'd spent trying to save his family had been lost on his mom. Marcus had endured a childhood of neglect and indifference, but he'd spent his adult life trying to help her. He checked on her in person once a week, called twice a week at least, and had offered time and time again to pay for any rehab she'd agree to attend.

It hadn't been enough. Why hadn't it been enough? He'd wanted her to pull out of the devil's grip so fiercely it ached, but for all his wanting, he couldn't save her. Why had he devoted his life to fixing cars instead of helping people like Tori?

The front door opened and blue lights flashed around Jake and another deputy as they entered.

Marcus caught Jake's attention and pointed to the room. "She's in here. We need paramedics."

Marcus pulled his brother out of the hallway so they could pass, and they moved to the couch where Meg, Trey, and Taylor sat with Dakota and Lindsey. He hadn't heard her come in, but he should have known Lindsey would be close behind her husband.

Lindsey pulled Brandon's arm until he turned to her. She opened her arms to him, and he continued crying against her neck as she hugged him.

Marcus turned to his other siblings and wrapped them in his arms together. His mission in life had been to protect them, and tonight felt like the ultimate failure. He didn't know for sure, but he assumed they'd all lost their mom tonight, and that was something he couldn't erase from their memories, especially Brandon's.

Sobs and gasping breaths filled the air, but he pulled them into a huddle and prayed aloud.

"Lord, if there's any hope left for our mom, please save her. Please guide Tori and the others as they try their best to help her." A lump clogged his throat, and he swallowed to clear it so he could continue.

"Lord, if tonight is her last on this earth, please be with us. Calm our hearts and help us find peace." His voice broke on the last word as Meg squeezed her arm tighter around his neck. If only he could give her the comfort she needed. No one deserved this, and he wouldn't wish it on his worst enemy.

His "Amen" was barely a whisper, and he felt dozens of tiny pricks behind his eyes when he opened them.

Turning, he saw Tori standing in the doorway with a look of dread on her face. He let out a shaky breath and wondered again why he couldn't save their mom. He'd prayed, he'd offered rehab, he'd kept a roof over her head, but it hadn't been enough. Would anything have been enough? Loraine had been a tortured soul his whole life, and he hadn't found anything in his almost thirty years that got through to her.

He hadn't even been able to save his siblings from this gut-wrenching pain. Now, he'd brought Tori into this, and he didn't know where to go from here. This wasn't the place for her. It wasn't a life he wanted to give her, and the ache of more loss could have split him in two.

CHAPTER TWENTY-NINE

Marcus

Marcus waited with Brandon in the hallway of the hospital hours later as Jake asked him questions about Loraine and what had happened. The story Brandon told sounded more like a nightmare, and Marcus hated that his brother had been forced to watch their mother die.

When Jake was finished with his questioning, the deputy turned to Marcus and shook his head. "I hate this for you." Brandon stepped away down the hall toward the room where Tori was waiting with the kids, and Jake watched him go and said, "No one should have to see what he saw."

Marcus nodded and looked at the floor. What was he gonna do now? Loraine wanted to be cremated, but beyond that, he felt like a lost ball in high weeds—useless and alone.

"I'm here for you and the kids. Natalie is too. Let us help."

Marcus nodded again and gave Jake two slaps on the back as he followed Brandon down the sterile hallway.

Trey was asleep next to Meg, and Meg was leaning on Tori with her eyes half closed. Tori stared at the news report on the television mounted in the corner, but her gaze was lost on the moving images. Brandon sat beside Taylor in a corner, and neither of them spoke.

Tori turned to him when he stepped close enough, and she stood to meet him. "How'd it go?" She wrapped her arms around her middle, and the serious look on her face caused a pit of sadness to settle in his gut. Could he just pretend this awful night hadn't happened?

He shrugged. "Fine, I guess."

Tori touched his arm and guided him toward the door. "Come on. Let's go get some coffee."

When they were out in the hallway, Marcus leaned his back against the cold stone wall and didn't speak. He wasn't in the mood for coffee, and he didn't know what to say. His world was imploding around him, and he was useless to stop it.

"Talk to me, Marcus. Don't shut down. I'm here to help however I can."

He shook his head. "I don't want you in this."

"I'll just help with the kids. Meg can stay with me some nights, and I'll find things to do with them to keep them busy during the day."

Marcus huffed and straightened against the wall. "Don't you get it? I said I don't want you in this. I've had enough, Tori. I'm done. I can't go around caring about everyone just so they can let me down!"

Anger roiled inside him. He wasn't mad at Tori, but he was furious at…something. Nothing that was happening was fair or right.

Tori shook her head and pulled her lips into a thin line. "Don't push me away. You're sabotaging the good that's left for both of us."

"Is this really good for both of us? What's in it for you? You wouldn't have signed on for this had you known what a mess my life really is when you met me."

"That's not true. I love you."

How could he have been so careless? Love meant getting hurt, and he hated the twisting that was prying his chest open. He'd only recently found out what love meant past God and his family, and it was being taken away from him too soon. He would throw it away to keep her from this pain.

"Go home, Tori."

"No."

Love had broken him. Love made getting through life unscathed almost impossible.

Love inevitably turned into pain, and right now, he was hurting enough to wonder if it was worth the risk.

He'd thought Tori would be the exception to the rule. He'd imagined he could love her without the hurt, but that would require feeling less, and half loving her was impossible.

"I need to get the kids home, and it's been a long night."

Tori's brows drew together, and she bit her bottom lip as her chin quivered. "This isn't over."

He was meant to sabotage any chance he had of connecting with someone, and he had to take it for what it was and move on. It wasn't fair to drag her down with him. He'd never been good enough before, and he still wasn't good enough now.

He couldn't stand this close to her any longer. He was empty, and the gulf of loneliness inside him reached up to take the last bit of hope he could have held onto as he stepped around her and back into the waiting room.

She didn't follow him, and part of him was glad. He needed time to get past the hurt, the madness he was feeling. He sat beside Meg, and when she stayed quiet, he knew she was feeling it too.

"You told her to leave, didn't you?" Meg whispered.

Marcus didn't respond. His sister wouldn't understand. Instead, he bowed his head and prayed silently. He talked to God, asked questions, and sorted out his confusing thoughts. When he raised his head, he rubbed his hands over his face and felt slightly calmer.

He'd hurt Tori tonight. She'd tried to save his mother, and he'd said the simple "Thank you" on the way to the hospital, but then he'd washed away everything they'd been building together.

The love he felt for her was real, but it was terrifying to accept it when the things he loved could be torn from him in an instant.

He knew he should make things right with Tori, if she'd even listen to him after tonight, but right now, his family needed him more.

Marcus pulled Meg closer and she cried quiet tears onto his shoulder. "I'm sorry," he whispered.

He listened to Meg's ragged breathing and wondered when he'd stop letting people down.

CHAPTER THIRTY

Tori

It had been almost a week since Tori had left Marcus and his family at the hospital. He hadn't answered her phone calls or texts, and he hadn't been at the shop on Tuesday when she'd stopped by to talk.

Her friends seemed to have a pact to trade off spending time with her to keep her mind off Marcus. Today, Lindsey was helping her wrap the last of the presents for the bingo game at the Christmas Eve party.

Surely, she'd see him then, if not before. She had gifts for him and the kids, and she was determined they would have them. Thinking about the plans she'd had to spend Christmas with the new family she'd come to love was breaking her apart inside again.

Marcus' words from the hospital rang stale and clinical in her mind. *"Go home, Tori."*

What if she didn't know where home was anymore? Tori had once thought Chicago was home, but she hadn't thought about the place in weeks, much less missed it. Years ago, she'd made a home in that city with Scott, but when it all fell apart, she hadn't wanted to fight to keep it. She *wanted* to fight for what she'd had with Marcus. In fact, she knew she wouldn't give up. She couldn't just walk away from what they had, and she knew, somewhere deep in her soul, that he couldn't either.

The thought of going back to Chicago with her tail between her legs wasn't an option. She'd made the decision to build her life here, and she would do it… *with* Marcus.

Tori even had a job here now. She'd gone in this morning to sign paperwork and tour the clinic. She'd been so eager to tell Marcus the good news, but she'd been swept up in their perfect date and forgotten until it was too late.

She watched Lindsey fluff a silver bow atop a present she'd just finished wrapping and wondered if she'd ever find her true home like Lindsey had. Tori knew her friend had walked a long road to find her happily ever after and thought maybe there was hope in time. Lindsey's journey had taken six years to circle back to her home in Carson with Dakota.

Could she wait six years for her own happily ever after? Tori taped the wrapping paper on a present and decided that she could. Marcus and his family were worth the wait.

Lindsey pushed the last wrapped gift into a pile with the others. "Done. I'm starving. What's for lunch?"

Tori stood and stretched her back. "I made chicken and dumplings last night. Sound good?"

Lindsey sat on the floor and drew a deep breath. "Perfect. As long as I don't have to get up. Nobody told me pregnancy was so exhausting."

"Don't get up. I'll fix our bowls, and we can eat right there."

Tori pulled the bowl of leftovers from the fridge and heard her phone ringing in the living room. "Hey, Lindz, can you get that?"

Lindsey said, "It's your mom."

"Just put it on speaker." Tori knew she could hear her mom from the open, connected kitchen.

Tori often talked to her mom while her friends were visiting now, and they'd been a part of many speakerphone conversations.

"Hey, Ms. Sanders, how are you?"

"Lindsey? I'm doing well. What about you? How is the pregnancy?"

Tori looked over the large kitchen island and saw her friend place a hand on her still-flat stomach. "It's amazing. I'm so excited, and our last appointment got a great report."

"That's wonderful. How's Tori doing?"

"You're on speakerphone, so she can hear you. She's right here in the kitchen."

Tori spooned the dumplings into a second bowl and said, "Hey, Mom."

"Sweetie, you sound better today."

Tori had been moping, and her mom was the one she'd vented to the most. Keeping a strong face was tough, but she could be herself with her mom.

"I'm okay."

"Still no word?"

"Not yet."

Lindsey leaned back and propped against the couch where she sat on the floor and said, "I don't think she's tried very hard. I know Marcus is spending time with his family, but she should just go to his house, right?"

Tori frowned as the microwave beeped. "I'm not going to his house. They're mourning."

"And so are you. I told him that just yesterday."

The spoon Tori had been holding gave a loud ting against the bowl as she dropped it. "You talked to him?"

"Yeah, he's havin' a really tough time. He knows he messed up, but he's afraid of what he's done."

Tori didn't say anything as her mom and Lindsey continued talking. Didn't he realize she was scared too? He understood her better than anyone, except her mother, and he knew losing the people she'd finally connected with would be heartbreaking for her. He'd been patient as she adjusted to the changes going on in her life, and he'd been pivotal in her growing relationship with Christ. Not one bit of their relationship was disposable, and she couldn't let it go.

Lindsey continued chatting with Mom. "Marcus is so broody. I don't know how those two made it work, but they did! I've never seen him so happy."

Tori spoke up as she handed Lindsey her bowl and a napkin. "He's special, and he understands me like I understand him." It wasn't hard to know the truth of Marcus' heart. The connection she felt with him was true and trusting.

Her mom spoke up, "Baby, you've got to talk to him. I've seen you grow with him and your friends since you moved there, and I want that happiness for you."

"I know, but he won't talk to me."

Lindsey sat forward with a mischievous smile. "Then make him."

Tori laughed. "I've been trying."

"Not very hard. Go to the shop again today. I bet he's there. Marcus is a loner, and it's against his nature to seek someone out." Lindsey looked at her watch then spooned another bite of chicken and dumplings into her mouth.

Tori pinched the bridge of her nose. "He doesn't want to talk to me. If he did, I would have heard from him."

Lindsey shook her head. "I wouldn't lead you on if I wasn't sure. He's been grieving, and grief changes people. But I've seen him, and he *does* love you."

Tori had already decided to keep trying to talk to him, but the rejection was like being kicked while she was down. "Okay. I'll try again."

"Tori, I hope things can work out between the two of you. I'll be there in a few days, and I can't wait to see you," her mom said.

"I can't wait to see you too, Mom."

They said their good-byes, and Lindsey smiled. "So, you're going to see him today?"

"I don't know if I'll go today. Maybe I should just wait for the Christmas party."

Lindsey threw her head back against the couch. "I can't wait that long. It hurts seeing my friends unhappy."

"Yeah, well, it hurts being on this side of the breakup too."

Tori's phone rang again, and Lindsey leaned over to check the screen and said, "It's Scott! Don't answer that. You told him not to call you again."

Nervousness pooled in Tori's stomach as she stared at his name on the screen.

"Actually, can we put it on speakerphone?" Lindsey asked.

"Lindsey, you're so nosy."

"I'm just curious about what he could possibly be calling about. He was a jerk the last time you spoke."

That was true, and she'd told him not to call.

Tori answered the call and wondered if she was making a mistake. "Hello."

"Victoria? It's Scott. How are you?"

At least he didn't seem angry. "I'm okay." The petty side of her refused to ask him how he was doing. She didn't want to know.

"I-I don't know why I'm calling, really."

The seconds passed slowly as she waited for him to say more, and she realized she didn't feel any anger toward him anymore. She'd moved on so completely, that whatever he said or did couldn't faze her anymore.

"It's Christmas, and I wanted to make sure you're all right, I guess."

Tori couldn't reply, because anything other than "I'm not okay" would be a lie.

"And I wanted to tell you I'm sorry for the way I acted. It seems like you're happy now, and really, I am too. We shouldn't be fighting, and I wanted to clear things up as best I could."

She took a moment to let the cleansing breaths wash away her muddled thoughts. "I'm not angry with you anymore. We wanted different things, and we've found what's right for both of us now."

He didn't need to know that she'd found her happiness then lost it.

Scott said, "It wasn't fair to you that I changed and wanted something different while we were together."

"I understand change more than you know." The conversation was upsetting her, and Lindsey reached for her hand as she continued.

"Well, I just want to say that I hope you like it there. You know I grew up in that cabin."

"I do now. I didn't know that when we were married."

"I should have told you, but I didn't like talking about it."

"It's water under the bridge." She needed to end this call before her emotions got the better of her. She was missing Marcus, and she wanted to lean on Lindsey's shoulder and cry her losses away.

"Small-town life isn't for me, but it seems to suit you. I wish you well."

"Thank you." Her replies were clipped now, afraid a betraying sob would escape.

"Merry Christmas, Victoria."

"Merry Christmas to you too. Good-bye."

Tori hung up the call, and Lindsey's arms wrapped around her neck. "Are you okay?"

"I've been better. I miss Marcus and my family."

Lindsey rubbed her back and said, "I know you're not feeling very strong right now, but I really wish you'd go talk to him."

"I don't know how much longer I can go without seeing him anyway."

"Does that mean you'll go?"

Tori raised her head and wiped her eyes. "Yeah, I'll go."

CHAPTER THIRTY-ONE

Marcus

Marcus twisted the wrench and strained against the unforgiving bolt. Instead of breaking free, his knuckles went skipping across the uneven surfaces under the car.

"Ahh!" He let the wrench fall to the concrete floor with a clink and pulled his throbbing hand to his stomach and squeezed.

His string of terrible days was growing longer, and he wondered when he'd be able to breathe again without hurting. He was gasping for air, but no matter how hard he tried, his lungs never felt satisfied. It was as if the air he was breathing wasn't good enough anymore. He was just surviving where he'd been thriving before.

Before his mother died. Before he royally messed up everything with Tori.

Marcus had known better than to get invested in something so beautiful. Tori was so far out of his league he couldn't even see her, and he'd fallen for her anyway only to drag her through the mud of his life.

He wasn't made for nice things, and he'd let it all fall apart—as it was meant to do.

As if he needed another factor to grate on his nerves, the song on the radio changed to some new teenybopper repetitive junk, and Marcus screamed. The release of his anger echoed off the small space beneath the car, and he was glad he was alone in the shop.

Marcus did it again, screamed until his throat ached, and it didn't make a dent in his frustration. Nothing could touch the self-loathing he'd been carrying this past week.

He couldn't stand that noise another minute. Sliding out from underneath the car in a rush, he wiped the blood from his knuckles and stumbled to the radio and turned it off. The silence that engulfed the shop in the next instant was only interrupted by his angry breathing.

Slumping down into a chair beside the wall, he rested his elbows against his knees and put his head in his hands. What he wouldn't give to talk to Tori right now, to feel her arms around him, to hear her whisper those assurances in pretty words he would believe without thinking twice.

He'd been so wrong, but maybe a little right. He wanted better for her, but he wished with everything he had that he could be enough for her.

He had to see her, needed to apologize. She needed to know how sorry he was for hurting her and pushing her away. He hadn't meant it.

Marcus stood and heard gravel crunching outside the only open garage bay. The last thing he wanted was a customer. He wasn't in the mood to see anyone except Tori right now. His customer service persona was officially on vacation until further notice.

Marcus stood and made his way toward the opening as he heard a car door slam. "We're closed." The sun was setting and an orange glow shrouded the parking lot.

A woman stepped into the bay opening, and the bright rays shone around her, casting a shadow over her face. A jolt hit his heart, and he was reminded of the reason he called her angel.

It didn't matter; he didn't have to see her face to know her. He'd recognize her by any one of her defining characteristics. Her glowing blonde hair, the way she walked, the clothes she wore—everything about her was a significant part of her that he loved.

Another wave of anger coursed through him as he stood admiring her. The last thing he needed right now was to be reminded of how much he ached to be with her when he wasn't sure if she was here to talk or scream at him.

In the same moment, he was acutely aware of how unattainable she was to him. His anger was raw and too fresh, but never directed at her.

He couldn't speak. He just stood staring at her, letting the rip in his chest grow wider and gaping with every second.

"Hey," she finally said and took a step toward him.

He still couldn't move.

"Can we talk, please?"

He nodded and led the way to his office. Once inside, he realized he didn't want a desk sitting between them. He didn't even want the air floating between them, but there were some things he just couldn't have.

Maybe he'd used up all his happiness in those few weeks he'd been able to love her freely. Maybe each person was allotted a certain amount of goodness in their life, and once it was gone, there couldn't be any more. What if his love for her had burned so fiercely and so quickly that it had spent his entire life's happiness in a few months?

"I tried calling you," she whispered as he leaned against the wall in his office and offered her the clean chair he reserved for her.

"I know."

"That's all you have to say? Marcus, why are you pushing me away?" Her pitch was high, and he knew she was already worked up.

He rubbed his greasy hands through his hair and sighed. For once, he didn't know what to say. He couldn't promise her things would get better. He didn't know that. He'd been working hard to make a good life for his family for ten years, and they still didn't have it all worked out.

Tori spoke, and her words were like a salve on wounds. "I don't know what you're going through right now because you won't tell me. If you'd just let me in, I could help you. We could get through this together."

Marcus scratched the stubble that coated his cheek. He was scared of what she'd say and ashamed of what he'd said.

Tori stood and the fire in her blue eyes was burning white hot. "You're just scared because you don't know what's going to happen, and you're afraid of what we could be together."

He knew what that scene would look like. Him dragging her down every chance he got and a life full of wishing he could be *more* for her.

"But I'm scared too, and I'm afraid I'm losing you." Her voice cracked on the last word, and he swallowed the burning in his throat.

Was she saying she really wanted this with him? Why was she always so good with words, and he couldn't conjure any when he needed them so badly?

"You told me you'd always come for me when I was scared. Those storms, those times when I was scared and you came for me, they brought us together."

She took a step toward him, and he ached to reach out and wrap her in his arms.

"This is your storm, Marcus. Your fear is losing the people you love, and you need to learn to count on me to come running for you when you need me."

He looked into her eyes and rocked back and forth against the wall at his back. "You don't understand." The injustice felt like the loss of something vital, like a heart or a brain, and he wished for something that he couldn't touch.

"I do understand. I know you too well not to understand."

"I can't give you anything."

"I don't care!" She screamed the words into the small office and stepped closer to him. "Do you hear me? I don't care. I can make my own decisions, Marcus, and I'm staying here." She jabbed a finger toward the floor to emphasize just what she meant by *here*. "I care too much about you and your family."

There she was, his fiery angel. The one he couldn't live without. The one he would spend every day of his life loving to the fullest.

Marcus erased the small space between them and wrapped her in his arms. He was filthy, but he couldn't stop himself from smothering her in his embrace. He'd have her entire wardrobe replaced just to hold her in this moment.

"I need you. I love you. I'm so sorry," he whispered in her ear.

"I want a lifetime of what you've shown me here, and I'm not leaving you. Ever."

He was rocking from side to side, and the movement was comforting. He wondered if that's why babies were soothed when they were rocked in the arms of someone who loved them.

Marcus swallowed and said, "I know you're not. I didn't mean what I said at the hospital. I was scared and mad at everything, except you. I don't ever want to hurt you, and I did. I'm sorry."

His hand rested on her back as he hugged her tight, and he felt the uneven breaths before she spoke.

"My marriage was a way of running from my fears. I couldn't see it at the time, but I was afraid that if someone really saw me, the real me, and I opened up and gave my heart to someone…" She paused, and he gripped the back of her neck and buried his face in her hair.

"I was afraid I wasn't worth the effort to stick around. My dad didn't think so." The floodgates broke, and her sobs came rushing out as if they were tripping over each other in their haste to be set free.

"No. That's all wrong." He held her tighter and she sobbed harder. "It's not true. I love you."

What had he done? He'd hurt her worse than he'd ever realized. How could he have been the one to make her feel so unworthy?

Marcus said, "I don't want you to ever feel that way. We're going through a hard time right now, but…" He searched his mind for words that held enough weight to carry the feelings he had for her. "I don't want to lose you. Not ever. You're right. As long as we're fighting on the same side, together, we can make it through anything."

He pulled her face away from his chest to look into her eyes. "I do know what we could be together. I don't want to miss a minute of us. I'm sorry I pushed you away. I never wanted to. I *am* scared. I know what love is. At least, now I do. I've known since you walked into my life."

Tori's blue eyes were red-rimmed and her face was wet, but she nodded.

"I haven't been the same since I met you, Tori. I love you, I want you, I need you, and I've never experienced any of those things before you."

She nodded again, and a strangled sound came from her throat.

"I love you, Tori. I'm so sorry."

"I-I got a job." Her words were rushed, and she cupped her hand over her mouth once they were out.

"Really? Where?"

"At a family clinic in town. It has good hours. I can pick up the kids from school."

He would never question the Almighty God that led this wonderful woman to him, but he'd forever wonder what he'd done to deserve someone so good. She cared about his family as much as he did, and that was something he'd never hoped to find.

All those prayers he'd been afraid to bring to life had been answered in Tori. Anyone who ever ended up with him would have to accept his family for what it was, and he was happy to let it be her.

He rested his head against her forehead. "You changed me, angel."

"I don't want to change you. I liked you from day one."

"I meant in good ways. I've never trusted anyone else with the important things in my life. I lived my life questioning everything and everyone. Now, I know it's a good thing to let someone in. You taught me that."

She leaned back looking confused. "I thought that's what *you* taught *me*. I had a conversation with my mom when I first arrived here about that exact thing."

"Looks like we're made for each other."

"I think we could be a pretty good team." She grinned, and he wiped her tearstained cheeks.

Marcus said, "I know I'm hard to love, but I'll always try to be my best for you."

"Same." She nodded and her grin grew into a full-on smile.

He'd almost lost her, and she'd come storming into his life, again, and put them back together. He was a mess without her, and he knew, now more than ever, that losing her wasn't an option.

CHAPTER THIRTY-TWO

Marcus

Marcus watched Lindsey link her arm with Tori's across the messy living room. Wrapping paper, bows, and boxes covered every inch of the main room floor in Dakota and Lindsey's house, and Marcus stuffed another wad of trash into the black garbage bag he carried.

They'd eaten, played bingo, and opened all the gifts before he'd gotten Lindsey alone to ask her to distract Tori so he could talk to her mother.

Now was his chance. He searched the room and found Tori's mom accepting a glass of apple cider from Barbara in the kitchen. It was Christmas Eve, and he and Tori had agreed to exchange their gifts tonight.

Passing the trash bag to Declan, he side-stepped piles of unwrapped presents as he sought out the woman he needed to talk to.

"Ms. Sanders, can I talk to you for a minute?"

Her eyes were the same color as Tori's, but her smile was smaller and more childlike.

"Of course, I've been hoping for some more time with you."

Her plane had landed yesterday, and Marcus had been able to ride with Tori to Atlanta to pick her up. Marcus had talked more during that car ride than he had in the last year, but Tori's mom was sweet and curious about him. How could he have denied her the answers she requested?

Marcus led her to a hallway off the opposite side of the room where Lindsey and Tori had gone. "I wanted to show you the Christmas present I got for Tori."

Tori's mother covered her cheeks with her hands. "Please! Let me see."

He pulled the box out of his coat pocket and opened it for her. She gasped and placed a hand in front of her mouth, and with only her eyes exposed, she could have passed for Tori's twin.

Letting her hand fall from her mouth to rest on his arm, she said, "She'll love it, Marcus. It's perfect."

"You sure?"

The gentle squeeze on his arm was the trigger releasing the smile he'd been trying to contain.

"Of course, I'm sure." Tori's mother wrapped her arms around his neck and a wave of thankfulness washed over him.

He was grateful God had seen fit to give Tori a wonderful mother. Not everyone was so fortunate, but a world where Tori would have been forced to endure the neglect he had his whole life would have broken something important inside him.

Marcus pulled away from her and tucked the box back into the inside pocket of his coat. "We need to get back out there. I just wanted to show you before I gave it to her."

"You're right. I wouldn't want her catching us and wondering what we're up to." Tori's mother winked at him.

"We'll find you again in a little while."

"Don't worry about me. I'm having fun with my new friends." Tori's mom walked off to sit with some of the other ladies.

Marcus returned to his task of picking up the Christmas party mess while he waited for Lindsey to bring Tori back. Now that her mom had seen it, he couldn't wait to show Tori.

He heard Tori's laugh before he saw her. Lindsey doubled over in laughter in the hallway entrance as Tori wiped her eyes as her laugh continued in bursts when she could catch her breath.

"What's so funny?" Marcus asked with one eyebrow raised.

Tori attempted to fix her makeup once again. "Lindsey told me about the time Dakota got a bee up his shorts and pulled them off and ran screaming into the pond." Tori's laughter renewed as her face turned red.

"Come on, ladies. Give the man a break. He was ten!"

Lindsey waved her hand in front of her face. "Doesn't matter. It was hilarious, and I'll never forget it."

Marcus agreed. They'd all spent the next month taking turns reenacting Dakota's high-knee run into the pond.

"You're right. It was funny." He turned to Tori and wanted to laugh with her. Her belly laughs were contagious. "Let's grab some cider and sit on the porch for a little bit. It's a good time to exchange our gifts while the kids are occupied."

Marcus' brothers and sister had come with them to the party tonight, but he and Tori had agreed the kids couldn't have their presents from the two of them until Christmas morning. He'd told Tori earlier he'd be bringing her gift to the party tonight so they could exchange them alone.

Tori winked at him and turned to Lindsey. "I'll catch up with you later."

They each grabbed a cup of cider, and Tori ran out to her car to get his gift. He grabbed her own gift from the guest bedroom where it was hidden and waited on the porch for her until he noticed how big the gift was Tori struggled to carry.

Running to help her, he said, "I got it," and took the bulky gift wrapped in red paper with white snowflakes from her hands.

"It's not heavy; it's just big."

"We could have done this at your house. I hate that you brought this all the way here." The present was long, wide, and thin, and the shape was cumbersome.

"I wanted you to see it tonight. I can't wait for you to open it, but before you do, I have to tell you that Meg put just as much into this as I did."

Meg was a teenager, and he knew how easily her friends and peers at school could influence her. Knowing she'd been spending her time with Tori instead of getting into trouble made him proud of his sister and the woman she was becoming.

"Can I open mine first?" Marcus asked as he set the bulky present down on the porch beside the swing.

The sky was midnight blue, and the moon was bright enough to outshine the stars. Tori sat in the swing on the porch and braced her feet against the floorboards to keep it still so Marcus could sit.

"Sure. I can't wait." Tori pulled her coat tighter around her body and shivered. They were expecting snow flurries tomorrow, but tonight, there wasn't a cloud in the sky.

Marcus tore the wrapping from the gift and squinted against the dark night to see.

Tori said, "It's a collage." She pointed to tickets in the corner of the frame. "These are from the fair."

Then she pointed to a photo of Trey when he was no older than three. "That's my favorite."

Marcus studied the photos, cards, and tickets that filled the board, overlapping in abundance. It was all here. The people he loved and the happiness they'd shared was locked inside this frame.

"Do you like it?"

"Tori, I love it. No one has ever given me something like this before."

Tori leaned her head on his shoulder and stared at the mass of photos he couldn't look away from. "Look how happy they are."

She was right. Every photo was bursting with smiles and joy.

"You did that," she whispered.

He'd been so worried about not living up to the job of their guardian to see that they *had* been happy. They didn't have riches, but he loved them with every ounce of his soul.

"Thank you. I love it."

Tori kissed his cheek and asked, "Where's mine?"

Marcus handed her a heavy, rectangular box with sharp edges wrapped in navy-blue paper with snowmen on it. "Merry Christmas."

Tori looked at him as if she expected him to tell her what lay waiting inside the box as she reached for it.

Marcus watched her unwrap the gift with enough care that she didn't tear the paper. He'd never seen anyone so gentle and patient with a present.

Tori lifted the box and read the words printed on the front. "New King James Bible."

She lowered the box to her lap and cradled it in both hands as she stared.

He tried to read her face, but the angle cast her features in darkness. His heart sank thinking she wouldn't like it.

"I noticed you use that Bible Barbara gave you a few weeks ago, so I got you one of your own. It has your name monogrammed on the front."

Tori opened the box and looked for her name, but he reached to open the front cover before she could see it. "It has a family tree in the front. I thought it could be our family Bible."

At last, she looked up at him, and her mouth hung slightly open for a moment before she spoke. "Family?"

He closed the cover of the Bible, and she read her name on the front. "Victoria."

She traced the letters of her given name with her fingertips. "Marcus, I love it. I've been meaning to get one for weeks. Thank you. This is exactly what I wanted." Her voice cracked on the last word, and she cupped her hand over her mouth and continued staring at the leather cover.

"I left the last name off… for now."

She turned back to him and tilted her head. "Why?"

"I have another gift for you." He pulled the small box from his pocket and knelt in front of the swing.

Tori gasped and, this time, both hands covered her mouth.

"Tori, I love you with everything I have, and I promise to love you for the rest of my life. Will you marry me?"

"Yes! Yes, I will." Tori pulled him from where he knelt before her to stand with her. "Yes, I want to marry you. I want to be your wife."

Her arms were locked around his neck, and he held her body close.

She whispered in his ear, "I love you."

Marcus pulled away enough to look into her eyes for only a moment before pulling her in for a kiss. Her lips were soft and urging as he deepened the kiss and let every happiness she'd given him flow through him. Holding her close, he thought the love he held for her would light up the night.

When she pulled back and gasped to catch her breath, her gorgeous smile made him ache to kiss her again.

"Let's get married now," she said.

He laughed, but her words struck a familiar chord in him. "When?"

"Now."

He pulled her waist closer and rested his forehead against hers. "I don't think the courthouse opens until after Christmas. We can't get a license tonight, angel."

"Then right after Christmas, while my mom is still in town. I want her to be here. Our friends can help us put it together!"

Marcus laughed. "You're crazy."

"No, I just know this is what I want, and I don't want to wait. I love you, and I want to be your wife."

Marcus thought for a moment. "The church is decorated for Christmas. We could just ask them to leave it up a few days after and we could get married there."

Tori nodded and continued, "We could get a dress for me and bridesmaid dresses for the girls the day after Christmas. I can call that place where Lindsey got hers and see if we could just make an appointment to get them all in one day."

Marcus arched a brow. "I thought it took a long time to get dresses like that."

Tori shook her head. "We'll just buy them off the rack, and I'll pay extra to have anything altered overnight. If we're not spending a lot of money on a big wedding, we can make it quick."

"What about the men?" Of all things, he never imagined he'd be talking to his fiancée about groomsmen. Yet, here he stood, more than happy to jump as fast as he could into a marriage with the one woman in the world who understood him and loved him enough to spend her life with him.

"I don't care what they wear. As long as I'm your wife by the end of the week, I'm happy."

Marcus rubbed his calloused hand against his cheek. "Are you sure you don't want a nice wedding? You can take the time and plan it like you want."

"No." Tori shook her head. "This is what I want. Is that okay with you?"

"Do frogs eat flies?"

Tori laughed. "I promise I can do this. It'll be simple, but perfect. Just our friends and family in our church at Christmas."

"Tori, I swear we'll make any wedding you want happen. Are you sure this is what you want?"

"Yes! I had a big wedding before, and it didn't mean anything. Our wedding will be the beginning of our life together, and I want to stand with you in front of God and tell all of our friends and family how much I love you, then I want to spend the rest of my life with you."

Their life together. That thought alone sent shivers up his spine.

"We haven't talked about where we'll live, but I'd love it if you and the kids would move into the cabin. If you don't like it, we can find another place, but there's enough room for everyone to have their own room."

He started to speak, but she cut him off.

"Wait, I've thought about it a lot. I don't owe anything on the cabin, and we could sell your house. It's old, but you've taken care of it. Plus," she paused as if afraid to continue. "I just think the kids would like to get away from the memory… of that night."

Tori was right. Brandon had been sleeping on the couch and he barely walked into the room to grab clothes, and Marcus had struggled with helping his brother cope with the things he'd seen.

"That sounds perfect. Are you sure?" Everything she'd suggested was logical and, well, as perfect as he'd claimed, but he wanted to make sure she got exactly what she wanted as they started their new relationship.

"I'm sure. I love the house and the river. The view is amazing, and it's… quiet. I never thought I'd enjoy living so close to nature when

I've always lived in the city, but it's nice to be able to sit outside with my coffee in the mornings and watch the birds on the water. I want that forever… with you."

"I want that too." He ran his fingers through the soft waves of her blonde hair.

"We're going to be a family." She smiled and made a sound that resembled a giggle. "You can drop the kids off at school on your way to the shop, and I can pick them up from school on my way home from work. It'll be perfect."

After the loss his family had suffered, he couldn't wait to share the news with them. "We still have to tell the kids."

"Let's wait until tomorrow. I want it to be a Christmas surprise."

"Good," Marcus whispered as he leaned in until his lips nearly brushed against hers. He could smell the cider and ginger on her breath. "Let's enjoy the night. You'll only be my fiancée for a few days."

Tori's head was tilted up to look at him, and her eyes were unguarded. He saw her love, her trust, and her passion in those blue irises.

"Channing," she said. "Tell them to write Victoria Channing on the Bible, please."

He kissed her then and sealed the promise of their lifetime together.

$\mathscr{E}$PILOGUE

Tori
Three Months Later

Tori stepped onto the porch into the bright glow of the spring sunrise. She'd spent almost every morning watching this sunrise, and every day she looked forward to the next. Each dawn was different in color and shade and weather, and she cherished the gift God gave her to start each day.

This morning, she walked to the rail cradling her mug of hot coffee and looked to the sky. She could just make out the round moon hanging high above the trees that were just waking up from the harsh winter. It was rare that she caught a glimpse of the moon in the morning, but she always enjoyed the novelty. It hung inconspicuous and hazy white against the soft-blue sky.

The sun, trying to take its proper place in the sky against the moon's wishes, lit up the rushing river that spilled over the bank meant to contain it. A storm had rolled through last night, and the river was lively and overfilled.

Despite the storm of the night before, not a single cloud dared to mar her view this morning.

Marcus had rolled into her life like a thunderstorm, and in that uncertainty of their beginning, she'd feared him to the marrow of her bones. She was afraid of the damage he could cause, the destruction he could leave behind after changing her and opening her heart to love and the life she could have here.

Now, she had weathered the storm of their new beginning, and she could see Marcus for what he really was to her—a spring rain made to nurture and make everything new. Her relationship with Marcus was something to be appreciated and welcomed after a barren winter.

Tori breathed in the untouched morning air and sat content in the knowledge that this beauty was her home. This home she had fought to claim as her own meant more than any luxury loft in Chicago. It wasn't the Wright House anymore; it was *their* house.

She knew what it meant to wake up next to the one you loved in a house full of family. She'd learned how to cherish the moments that made her heart soar right alongside the times they'd walked away from disaster hand in hand.

They were married two days after Christmas in the beautifully decorated church surrounded by the ones who loved them. Marcus and his siblings had moved into the house over the Christmas break when the kids were out of school, and in a matter of weeks, her cabin on the river had become the home she'd always wanted.

Trey, Taylor, and Megan were happy to have their own rooms, but Brandon had been a challenge. Not even the new home could shake his sadness.

Football season was over, and Marcus and Tori searched for anything to lift Brandon's spirits. They offered counselors and met with teachers, but Brandon wasn't ready to let go of their mother's passing.

After a month of worrying, Tori had suggested Brandon go to work with Marcus to have something to do. No one had expected the series of changes that occurred after that day. Brandon had watched Marcus work on the cars for weeks before he started talking again, but only to ask questions about the mechanics.

A month later, Brandon had come to Marcus and Tori to ask if he could work at the shop with Marcus after he graduated until he figured out what he wanted to do with his life.

Marcus had agreed instantly, but they both assured him he could go to college if he wanted. They would pay his way as soon as he was ready.

Brandon had accepted the job and promised to keep his mind open to other jobs and even college.

After the talk with Brandon that day, Marcus and Tori had gone to bed that night thankful their prayers had been answered for Brandon to find his way. He was still deciding, but they were confident Brandon was on the right track now. Once he took the job at the shop, Marcus and Tori had made a point to buy a starter car for Brandon, and he paid half the payment each month.

Tori's heart was satisfied now that Brandon had found something that he enjoyed again. She hadn't expected to learn so much from every experience her new family brought into her life, but the tough times were just as important as the happy times.

Thinking back on the change that brought her here to this place, she realized she couldn't have expected the decisions that would lead her to this fate. She hadn't known the path God had chosen for her, but now, she welcomed it with open arms.

Tori began her morning prayer and let the wind brush against her cheeks.

The door behind her creaked, and she knew Marcus was coming to join her. A morning as beautiful as this one should be shared, and she ended her prayer by thanking God for allowing her to share more than just the morning with her husband.

She opened her eyes and didn't turn to him as she waited for him to join her. She'd traded her tiring hours of work for cherished moments of fun and laughter with Marcus, his family, and their friends. Each minute felt precious, and she was happy to be surrounded by people who loved her.

Marcus set his coffee mug on the porch's banister and she felt his warmth at her back as his arms wound around her waist.

His breath tickled her neck as he whispered, "I love you."

"I love you too," she confessed into the quiet morning. "And I love this place."

Marcus took a deep breath as he leaned his cheek against her hair. "I know this might look like the middle of nowhere, but—"

Tori squeezed his arms that encircled her like a warm blanket as she finished his thought. "It's right in the middle of where I want to be."

ABOUT THE AUTHOR

Mandi Blake was born and raised in Alabama where she lives with her husband and daughter, but her southern heart loves to travel. Reading has been her favorite hobby for as long as she can remember, but writing is her passion. She loves a good happily ever after in her sweet Christian romance books and loves to see her characters' relationships grow closer to God and each other.

Thank you so much for reading *Beautiful Storm*. I'm incredibly thankful for your support. I love writing books because I'm an avid reader myself. If you loved the book, stay tuned for more in the Unfailing Love series.

If you want to connect with me, visit my website here: www.mandiblakeauthor.com.

Made in the USA
Coppell, TX
24 November 2019

11848783R00182